BREATHE DEEP & SWIM

JENNA MARCUS

Distribution & Design by Bublish, Inc.

ISBN: 978-1-647043-13-1 (Paperback)
ISBN: 978-1-647043-12-4 (eBook)

*To my dad, Alan Marcus, for his infinite support,
and for listening to every chapter as I crafted this book.
Your generosity, compassion, and humor are priceless.
I would not be who I am without you.*

CONTENTS

ONE

NOT MIDNIGHT

It felt like a phantom clock was striking midnight.

I thought I heard twelve chimes, but maybe they were ringing somewhere off in the distance. Maybe I was just imagining it because the sound of midnight—that finite clang—would have fittingly stamped this moment. But even without hearing the distinctive ringing of a midnight bell, even without confirmation of the time, I'd always remember this moment. At some point in the night, Dad had died, and we'd been left to figure out the rest of our lives, or at least the next few hours.

I'd never seen a corpse before, not in its organic form, before being preserved in a coffin—only after being coiffed and cleaned to a perfection that never replicated the actual living person I once knew.

At Uncle Earl's funeral, he'd worn an intensely black suit with a matching tie, but he'd once said he would rather die than wear one. Well, I guess the suit was fitting then, because if he'd taken one look at that Windsor knot, he would have dropped dead on the spot.

Lying in that shiny coffin, Uncle Earl had been like a wax statue, a pristine, unnatural representation, not the Uncle Earl we knew. That wax figure wouldn't ruffle my hair while saying, "When are you going to cut that thing? Are you looking to grow a pet?" It'd always driven me crazy when he said that, but he was being true to who he was; he was his authentic self. In that coffin, any semblance of authenticity he'd once had dissipated, leaving a body in a proper suit. I supposed he'd been prepared and preserved to look like that for an audience, to appear "more palatable."

This was different though, and not because the dead man lying in the bed was my dad. This was different because my dad still looked like himself. He wasn't made up for anyone; his life had just faded away. His lily-pad-green eyes were dull and staring at nothing on the ceiling. His jaw was slack. He looked like he was waiting to sleep, but his soul had left his body instead.

The most potent difference was the absence of living movements. He was missing those subtle movements, like adjusting himself under the bedspread, or twitching his nose from time to time. He was missing his stare, when he would focus on a particular point as if to turn it over in his mind before slightly shaking his head to refocus his eyes. His dark-brown hair somehow had lost its sheen, which seemed impossible since it had grown oily from not showering for days on end.

It was his stillness that filled the room. His severe lack of movement connected him to all other corpses, but because he wasn't in the standard coffin, in the standard funeral home, I couldn't shake the expectation of seeing him move. It was almost like I was taking for granted that people *could* move. Even if you were a quadriplegic, your eyes could move back and forth, and your chest would rise and fall with every breath you took.

It was impossible to mistake a dead man for what he was, and however I felt about this situation, I *knew* that he was dead.

"Wolfgang, why is this door open?" Van Gogh called from the hall. His footsteps began to slow to a stop as he hesitated to enter the room. We both knew this room was off-limits, and we both knew why.

Normally I followed the rules, especially ones set by Van Gogh, but I'd felt compelled to go into our dad's room, almost as if…as if I knew that I would find my dead dad lying in his own filth. As I mentioned, it had been a while since he'd showered.

"Wolfgang, why are you in here? You know you shouldn't—holy shit!" Van Gogh shouted, stopping a few feet away from the bed.

Although my brother's eyes were usually a mirror image of our dad's lily-pad-green ones, his naturally seemed livelier. In fact, they seemed to be expanding and retracting, if that was even possible.

I had no idea how to respond, other than to say what we both knew was a lie.

"I don't know what happened. He just … died."

He just died. Yes, he had, that was obviously true, but we both knew what happened, we both knew the cause.

Van Gogh ran his fingers through his short dark-brown hair, staring down at the body.

"Shit, shit, *shit.*" My brother didn't always know what to say in uncomfortable situations, but that was probably because he was rarely uncomfortable. Even when he got into verbal boxing matches with Dad, he didn't seem uncomfortable, just angry and disgusted. But now, as he continued to run his fingers through his hair, it was obvious that he was severely uncomfortable.

"I know. I don't know what happened. I just found him here," I repeated. Normally, I was very verbose. It probably came from the fact that I was a bona fide bookworm, at least that's what my teachers told me. That was one of the reasons I did so well on my compositions, especially in English class. I usually knew how to sew together sentences that sounded articulate, but not obnoxiously so. Dad always said I was too smart for my own good, and that he couldn't understand a word I was saying—but that was because he wasn't really listening. He never really tried to understand.

"What are you even doing in here? You know you shouldn't be in here without a mask!" Van Gogh exclaimed, adjusting his white N95 mask.

"I mean, does it really matter anymore? He's dead," I said, reaching for the mask tucked in my back pocket.

"Wolfgang, we don't know if he's still contagious!" Van Gogh cried as he pulled a pair of gloves out of a pocket in his tattered Levi's. He handed them to me before helping me adjust my mask. "There, that's better."

We simultaneously looked down at the stiffening body. I didn't feel his skin, but I knew my dad's body was getting colder and that rigor mortis would set in at some point; it was only a matter of time. However, how much time we had, who knew? I couldn't tell you what time it was.

It was at that point that I asked the obvious yet complex question I knew was on both of our minds. "Now what?"

Van Gogh took a deep breath, so deep that I could feel him holding it for some time—as if he needed the oxygen, any oxygen, even if it were contaminated. He slowly exhaled as he looked over our dad's body.

"Now? We need to get out of this room," he said, taking hold of my hand and walking me into the hall. My brother hadn't held my hand since I was eight years old and he was ten. Even though Dad had never instructed Van Gogh to do so, he'd always taken hold of my hand as we walked across the street.

Although it was six years later, and I knew that as a high school freshman I was a little too old to walk hand in hand with my older brother, I was reluctant to let go. Van Gogh had always been my life raft. I knew I needed him, and I also knew I could always rely on him.

Although my brother's plans weren't always fully thought through, I knew he would have one. I knew he would do everything in his power to get us safely across that street.

When we were in the hall, Van Gogh released my hand and walked over to the couch, but he didn't sit down. Instead, he just walked around it, circling it like a vulture waiting for the right moment to land.

I pulled off my mask and tucked both the mask and the gloves into my back pocket. I couldn't help but watch my brother as he continued to circle the couch, looking down at the brown carpet.

"What should we do?" I just needed to ask this question. Van Gogh always knew what to do, even if he acted on a whim, which he usually did. Me, on the other hand . . . it took me forever to construct a plan. I had to think it through too much; I'd always anticipate the worst-case scenario and would end up scrapping fully formed plans. But not Van Gogh. No, he would just go with it and whatever happened, happened.

Also, my brother would take full responsibility for his actions, but he never seemed to regret them. For example, when he'd been caught tagging a wall when he was into graffiti art, he said that if Keith Haring could do it, why couldn't he? Granted, I'm sure Haring's younger brother didn't have to use his lawn mowing money to bail his brother out of jail, like I did. Even though our dad had yelled at him for a good hour about getting arrested and focusing more on his art than anything else, Van Gogh didn't seem remorseful. Although he never apologized to Dad for his actions, he did apologize to me because he knew that it had taken me a while to earn what became his bail money.

The following week, I'd found my money paid back with interest on my dresser. It was only later that I learned that my brother pawned some of his new art supplies to pay me back. I didn't even attempt to get them back because I knew that if I did, it would hurt his pride. We never spoke of the incident again because there was no need to; we were brothers. We would do anything for one another. That was just a fact.

For this reason, whatever decision Van Gogh made would affect the both of us, and he knew it. He normally worked well under pressure because he never let it get to him, but this was different. We both knew whatever decision he made would determine our fate. Nevertheless, he would figure out what to do. I didn't need to worry because whatever he decided, that was what we were going to do. Even if it wasn't the perfect plan, he would make sure it all worked out in the end. He always did.

I knew not to disturb my brother while he was thinking, so I calmly took a seat in the chair adjacent to the couch. I was tempted to pick up the book I'd left under the coffee table, not to read it but just to feel it in my hands. There was just something about holding a book, any book, that just put me at ease.

I eyed the spine, a cracked white crease severing the dull orange spine that read: *The **Catcher** in the **Rye**,* by J.D Salinger. You only needed to read the book once to know why the publisher chose to emphasize the words "catcher" and "rye" in the title, but I chose to read it about a dozen times, to the point where the annotations I jotted in the margins could be time stamped by the evolution of my penmanship. I really liked it when even the publisher would provide readers with a subtle hint about the book's deeper meaning. It was as if even those binding the book recognized its potential greatness.

As I was just about to lean forward to pick up Salinger's coming-of-age tale, Van Gogh stopped in his tracks. He turned toward me but didn't really see me. He seemed to be looking off in the distance, at an indiscriminate part of the wall. It could only mean one thing: Van Gogh had come up with a plan.

"Pack," he commanded. "Empty out our backpacks and pack everything we can carry," he said, marching toward our bedroom.

Pack? Following him into the bedroom, I watched him riffle through his canvas backpack, pulling out every textbook and notebook that he could find until the backpack was completely empty. I don't even think that he left a single pencil in there.

"Pack? Pack for what?" I questioned.

"We're leaving," Van Gogh stated, opening up his dresser drawer and pulling out a few pairs of socks and some of his boxers.

"We're leaving?" I sounded like an echo, mirroring his statements but recreating them into queries. "Why?"

"We have to," he stated, not looking up while continuing to shove his clothes into the backpack, trying to fashion it into a makeshift suitcase. "Damn, this may not be big enough."

"We have to?" Van Gogh didn't even bother to address that echo. He just walked over to my side of the room and emptied out my backpack.

"I know you're going to want to take some books, but don't take too many," my brother warned. "We're probably going to have to carry these backpacks for a while and if they're too heavy, we won't make it."

"We won't make it? Make it where?" Getting tired of my own questions, I shook my head, as if to reconfigure my brain, trying to prevent myself from being a parrot. "Van Gogh, where are we going? Why do we *have* to leave? What is the plan?" My questions came flooding out, a waterfall of inquiries that just seemed to spill out of me. I felt like I was talking a mile a minute, but I couldn't help it, my mouth was trying to catch up to my brain.

"Just pack first, ask questions later," he stated, punching down his clothes. "We need to make a list of essentials. What we *absolutely* need, not what we would like to have, okay?" Before Van Gogh could move toward our closet, I grabbed his wrist, giving it a firm hold.

At the touch of my hand, he finally looked into my eyes. His were a steady wash of green, with slightly dilated pupils, all nestled under a furrowed brow.

"Van Gogh, please, I need to know what's going on. Why are we packing?" I pleaded. "I'm not going to fight you on this, I never would, but I need to know what we are doing."

Van Gogh nodded, knowing me too well.

Although I would follow any plan my brother would put into motion, I needed to know the intricacies of the plan. This applied to anything, really. I had a habit of resisting something unless I knew *exactly* what was happening. For example, when I was little, I would scream when the dentist began to work on me because he had never explained what he was going to do before he stuck his instruments into my mouth. Apparently, I was screaming so much that the dentist was afraid to continue unless my dad agreed to having the dental assistants hold me down and give me a sedative. Although my dad agreed to this, Van Gogh yelled at the dentist when he heard the plan. Unfortunately, since Van Gogh was a kid himself, the adults won in the end.

Maybe it was that instance that caused me to hate doctors. I knew that we needed doctors to survive, especially now that we were in the midst of a global pandemic, but I just couldn't get over this underlying hatred. Well, actually, it wasn't that I hated them, but that I didn't trust them. I would always trust Van Gogh, though. I trusted him more than anyone else, so whatever we had to do, we were going to do it, but I just needed to know what *exactly* we were doing. I needed to make sense of it first.

Van Gogh took a deep breath and placed my now empty backpack on my bed.

"Wolfgang, we can't stay here. Pretty soon, the state will discover that Dad died. As far as I know, he is our only living relative in this state. Uncle

Earl was his only brother, who never had any kids, and Dad's parents died a long time ago, so it's just you and me. So, since there is no one who can take us in, we are now wards of the state, which means that we will be placed in foster care. I'm sixteen, so in the state of Florida, I am still a minor—if I were eighteen, it would be a different story, but I'm not. So, it's inevitable that we will go into foster care and then we will be separated. I know that you don't want that to happen, and neither do I, so our only choice is to run away."

Van Gogh's tone was so calm, but more than calm, it was steady. His tone was a stark contrast to my mind, which was still racing with questions and trying to process what he was telling me.

Words like "foster care" and "separated" kept flipping over and over in my mind. Was he right? Would we wind up in foster care? Would we be separated? He spoke as if he was speaking from experience. Even though I knew he'd never been in foster care, we did go to school with a few classmates who were not only in foster care, but who seemed to jump from home to home. Actually, to call the places where they lived a "home" was entirely inaccurate. They were more like temporary landing bases until they found a home—*if* they ever found a home. I did have one friend, Sophie, who'd found a permanent home with her foster family. Sophie said that she looked so much like her foster parents because they all wore the same black-framed glasses, and like her, her foster mom also had asthma. Although Sophie was adopted by a family that she loved, they'd adopted her when she was a lot younger than us, and she was not adopted with a sibling.

Van Gogh was right. Who was going to adopt two teenage brothers? It was a possibility, but we both knew that it was too slim. Van Gogh was right—we couldn't take that chance, we needed to leave. However, he still hadn't answered all my questions.

"Okay, but where are we running to? We have to be going somewhere, right?"

Van Gogh looked down at my hand, which was still gripping his wrist. When I let go, he placed both of his hands on my shoulders, and continued to look me right in the eyes. His gaze was even steadier than before, but his pupils seemed to retract a bit, so he looked more like his normal self.

"There's only one living relative I know about…our mom. I know that she ran away when we were both very young, but I remember Dad once mentioning that she lived in New York when they first met. It's a long trip but we have to make it. It's our only chance to stay together."

As I looked up into Van Gogh's eyes, I nodded, still processing the plan. Van Gogh always had a few inches on me. For this reason, although we were both pretty lanky, his hand-me-downs were always too long for me. I knew that if our dad was still alive, the blue T-shirt and matching jeans that Van Gogh was wearing would be passed down to me in a few months—but now who knew what would be passed down. Our dad was no longer alive to make those decisions, or any decisions at all. So now, we sought a new decision maker. Our mom.

Our mom. I had not heard that phrase in a long time. She left when I was three and Van Gogh was five years old. Dad never spoke about her and didn't keep any pictures of her in the house. I barely knew anything about her, except that she ran away and that she was the one who named us. I think that's why Dad felt the need to shorten our names to "Wolf" and "Van." He couldn't stand any memory of her in his house, and our names—*our existence*—were constant reminders of her imprint on his life.

"How are we going to get there?" I quickly pulled out my phone and did a search. "It's nearly 1,200 miles away, and we don't even know which part of New York she lived in," I stated, tucking my phone back into my front pocket.

I could feel Van Gogh's grip tightening a bit before he took his hands away from my shoulders and turned back to my empty backpack.

"The Bronx," Van Gogh stated, picking up my empty backpack and handing it to me. "She used to live on Pelham Parkway in the Bronx. So, that's where we're going—the Bronx, New York. Now, pack."

"How do you know that?"

Van Gogh shrugged as he looked at my backpack. "I just do."

"How are we going to get there?" I asked, feeling the weightlessness of my empty backpack.

"I have an idea. First, I need you to pack. We are wasting too much time," he said.

As he started pulling a couple of T-shirts and light sweaters off hangers, I took a look around our room.

I tried to relive that ubiquitous scenario when your house is on fire and you need to grab everything that is important to you. But I was coming up short.

Van Gogh didn't have to tell me that we would never return—that was a given.

As I scanned the room, I saw cracking white walls that really needed spackling. Aside from the cracks, the walls were dull and bare. In fact, essentially everything was bare. It was almost as if we lived a utilitarian lifestyle. The unmade beds and the clothes in both of our dressers and in the closet were the only signs that the room was lived in, but aside from my books and Van Gogh's art supplies, you would never know that *we* lived in this room.

Before packing any clothes, I decided to put on a few of the bulkier items so I could fit more books in my backpack. As we were nearing autumn, with the temperature cooling, I decided to pull on a sweater and wear my jean jacket over it. I was already wearing a pair of jeans, and my sneakers, so I thought I was wearing enough layers to be warm. Even though it was the middle of the night, I never bothered to change for bed. It was only at night that I could read my books in peace, without hearing Dad's cough reverberating throughout the house, or hearing him calling to Van Gogh to bring him something. With my dad's death, the house had become eerily silent, but I knew that even in this silence, I could never read here again. Van Gogh and I could never stand still here; we needed to keep moving.

I sized up my backpack and determined that I could take about ten paperback books, a few shirts, pants, socks and underwear. After I riffled through my dresser drawer and closet, I picked out my clothes and smooshed them down into the backpack.

As I scanned the bookcase, I noticed how engorged it was from years of hoarding books. Between the school letting us keep our paperbacks, birthday gifts from Van Gogh, and the library's weekly bookfairs, I genuinely had an abundance of books.

"Not too many," Van Gogh warned as he walked out of our bedroom. "I'm going to see what cash we have lying around."

Alone with my books, I determined that, like with my clothes, I could only take the essentials. But how do you determine which books are *essential?* They were all important to me, every single one, whether they were assigned or I'd chosen them myself. Each book carried a memory for me. I could tell you exactly when I read and reread each of the texts. Only a few were annotated, though. These were irreplaceable, so these would be the ones I needed to take.

I narrowed my selection down to seven essentials: S.E. Hinton's *The Outsiders;* Ray Bradbury's *Fahrenheit 451*; Chinua Achebe's *Things Fall Apart;* John Knowles's *A Separate Peace;* Amy Tan's *The Joy Luck Club;* Khaled Hosseini's *The Kite Runner;* and Jean-Paul Sartre's play, *No Exit.* Every single one of these texts had Post-its hanging out the sides and annotations in the margins.

After I put each book in my backpack, I zipped it up and swung it over my shoulder. Although it had more heft now, I could still fit a few extra items in there.

I quickly found J.D. Salinger's *The Catcher in the Rye* underneath the coffee table, unzipped my backpack, and added this to the collection.

I can fit a couple more books in here, I thought as I turned back to our bedroom. But before I could take another good look at the bookcase, I heard my brother calling for me down the hall, from Dad's bedroom.

"Van Gogh?" I questioned, as I inched into the room.

"I'm in the closet!" he yelled. I could see his feet sticking out of the open closet door as he was kneeling on the rug.

I diverted my eyes from looking at our dad's corpse, trying not to imagine it slowly deteriorating.

Van Gogh moved over so that we were both kneeling, looking into the closet.

"So, I was trying to find some money, and I think we hit the motherload," he said as he held a huge wad of cash in front of me. "There has to be over $1,000 here, easy. I'm sure there is more back here, we just need to look."

I nodded, still trying to process seeing that huge bundle of money. It was wrapped in a dingy, white rubber band, so Dad must have had that money for a while now.

"I checked his wallet too, but there was only about $20 in there. He had a few credit cards, but those are useless to us," Van Gogh said, as he sifted through a few pairs of shoes and pushed aside our dad's toolbox.

"Why is that useless? Do you think that they are maxed out?" If they were, that wouldn't surprise either one of us. Between paying the bills and our dad's growing bar tab, he had maxed out his cards a few times.

Van Gogh shrugged. "Maybe, but they are traceable. Once someone discovers his body, he will be in the system. If we were to use the credit card of a dead man, the card would be considered stolen, and the police would find us. At least if we use cash, the police can't trace us," Van Gogh reasoned.

"Well, they could trace the serial numbers," I noted.

Van Gogh smirked and shook his head. "You read too many detective stories. Hey, what's that?" he asked, pulling out a small, wooden box, buried deep in the closet. Before I could look at the box, I noticed that hidden behind the box was a stack of papers and two paperback books.

The papers seemed delicate and a little crumpled. In the middle of the papers, there was a photograph of a woman holding a swaddled baby. Before I could inspect the photo, my brother said, "This box is locked."

"What? Locked?"

"Yeah." He pointed out the small brass padlock dangling from the middle of the box. "I didn't see a key, though, did you?"

"No, but it doesn't look like you open it with a key," I said, pointing at the four small, metal loops jutting out from the bottom of the lock. Each loop had a set of numbers, zero through nine, etched into the metal. "It looks like a combination lock, but I've never seen one like this, have you?"

Van Gogh shook his head as he inspected the lock. "Maybe there's a slip of paper with the combination on it. Did you find anything like that?"

"No, but I did find this," I said, showing him the photo.

As my brother inspected the photo, he smiled. "Mom and you. Wow, I almost forgot what she looked like."

I'd completely forgotten what Mom looked like, as I stared at her shoulder-length, wavy light-brown hair and light-blue eyes. She was smiling down at the baby, who was apparently me. I couldn't have been older than a few weeks, maybe a few months.

Our dad never displayed any photos, let alone kept any of them, especially of our mom. It was almost as if he was trying to erase her existence from our lives because she left us. However, to our dad, she really left *him*.

"I also found these," I said as I handed Van Gogh the papers. He placed the box next to him as he carefully, but quickly, unfolded the papers. Once again, he smirked.

"You know what these are? These are our birth certificates."

I inched over to him to take a closer look. As we inspected the birth certificates, there was no surprising information. Granted, now I knew what the Mayor, Commissioner of Health, and the City Registrar's signatures looked like, but aside from this, the time of birth and the hospital in Florida were unsurprising. Mother: *Ann Miller*. Father: *Benjamin Stephen Thomas*. It all seemed pretty standard.

My gaze lingered on our full names though: *Van Gogh Vincent Thomas. Wolfgang Amadeus Mozart Thomas.* I couldn't help but wonder why Mom chose those names. Clearly, Van Gogh's name matched him perfectly. Although he never expressed a particular interest in post-impressionist art or the need to replicate *Starry Night*, he was unquestionably an artist. Maybe that's why "Van Gogh" was his first name. Mom had known that his artistic talents would emerge sooner or later. Maybe that's why she chose "Mozart" as one of my middle names. Perhaps she was questioning whether or not I would be a prodigal musician, like my namesake. By making "Mozart" my second—not even my *first*—middle name, it was almost as if she were planting the seed of musical genius, but she still doubted whether or not it would emerge. Perhaps she had been right in doing so because I couldn't play any instruments, and I enjoyed reading much more than I enjoyed trying to learn how to play music.

"I'll put the certificates in my bag. We may need these," Van Gogh said, as he pulled out his backpack and placed both the wooden box and our birth certificates inside. "Do you see anything else?"

"Just these books," I said, holding up the two paperbacks. One was too thin to be a novel. I inspected the orange cover with a black border, and what looked like an upside-down building with white smoke or clouds bleaching the orange cover and a tiny white airplane shooting out as if it was flying into the lower right border. I read the title to myself, *All My Sons* by Arthur Miller. "I wonder if he was related to Mom?" I muttered.

"What?" Van Gogh asked as he stood up.

"Oh, nothing. I was just wondering if Mom was related to Arthur Miller. I mean, they both have the same last name, but maybe that's a coincidence."

"I don't know. In any case, we need to leave soon. I'm going to see if I can find anything else. Meet me by the front door in a few minutes, okay?"

I nodded as Van Gogh left, leaving me to scan the other book cover. A lonely woman, who looked like she was from the Victorian age based on her attire, stared out at the reader with an expression of boredom. The title, *Madame Bovary* by Gustave Flaubert, hung over her head. Although I had heard of Arthur Miller, I had never read anything by Gustave Flaubert. As I tucked the books under my arm, and stood up, I couldn't help wondering why these books were in the back of our dad's closet—a man who rarely read. Despite not knowing who owned these books, I decided that these were the last two books that I would take with me.

TWO

STEALING A DEAD MAN'S CAR

"What now?" I asked Van Gogh, standing outside of our house. It was practically pitch-black, and it felt like the temperature had dropped quite a bit. Wearing layers was definitely the right choice.

I looked back at the house, as if trying to etch it into my memory. I don't remember living anywhere else other than the house our dad inherited from his parents. Uncle Earl already had a house, so when their parents died, they left their pale-green home to my dad and his new family. Maybe it was a home to them, but it never really felt like a home to me.

Oddly enough, I didn't feel a sense of attachment to the one-story, pale-green house. For the past fourteen years, I'd slept in the same room, read on the same dingy couch, and mowed the same patchy lawn. But it'd never really seemed like a *home* to me; it was more like a building where I could rest, read, and refuel. I once read a poem that began with the verse, "People are made of places." Perhaps this was the case for that poet, but I have to disagree. Maybe *some* people are made up of places, but it was difficult for me to believe that this house was a part of my identity. Maybe that's why I did not feel an ounce of sadness as I stood in front of the closed front door. This "place" wasn't a part of who I was. This was never my home. Van Gogh and I were each other's home. Nevertheless, we could not live on brotherhood alone.

Van Gogh dug into his front pocket and pulled out a set of keys.

"Now, we drive," he declared, walking toward the driveway.

"Drive?" I asked as he approached our dad's 1995 Pontiac Bonneville—another "inheritance" from his parents. The sea-green car was caked with grime and dirt from years of shunning car washes. When Van Gogh opened up the driver's side, you could see the tears in the beige interior from miles away.

"Get in," Van Gogh commanded as he pulled off his mask, flung his backpack on the backseat, and eased into the driver's seat.

Following suit, I slid into the front passenger's side, placed my N95 mask next to me, and tossed my backpack next to Van Gogh's, praying that the car would start.

"Do you really think this is a good idea?" I asked, as he fought to turn over the engine.

After a few more tries, Van Gogh muttered that he would give the car a minute. Then he gave it one more attempt, and as if sensing Van Gogh's determination, the car obeyed with the prompt rumble of the engine.

Van Gogh smiled as he shifted the gear into reverse and looked back at the dark, empty street as we backed out of the driveway.

We sat in silence for a beat before Van Gogh said anything.

"Did you bring your charger?" Van Gogh questioned as he gripped the beige steering wheel.

Charger! Damn! I'd known that I was going to forget something.

"Sorry, I forgot," I admitted.

"That's okay, I brought mine, but it's in my backpack. Can you pull up Google Maps?"

As I was scrolling through my apps, I repeated the question, "Do you really think this is a good idea?"

As my brother eased the car to a stop at a red light, he turned to me.

"We need to get to New York, right? As you said, it's around 1,200 miles away. I can't think of a better way to get there, can you?"

Although I felt there was probably an alternative to this plan, which did not involve us stealing our dad's car, I just nodded.

"Just take a deep breath and relax. Everything will work out," Van Gogh assured me, hitting the accelerator as soon as the light turned green.

Breathe deep and swim, I said to myself, as I closed my eyes and inhaled all of the oxygen that I could take in. I may not have remembered our mom's appearance, but I clearly remember that that was her phrase. Her voice was like honey pouring into my ears. "Breathe deep and swim," she'd advised. Although I clearly remember this statement, I don't remember being near a body of water. The setting is fuzzy and frayed, but I distinctly remember a lack of swim gear. No water, no inflatable, neon water wings, no swim trunks. I don't even remember being wet or preparing for this eventuality. However, that phrase had stirred a sense of comfort and assurance in me, especially in that moment. Maybe it was because *she* was the one who said it, or because there was something about that moment that I couldn't recall where that phrase would make sense—I didn't know. All I knew for certain was that she'd said this phrase directly to me, and that this was my only memory of her.

Breathe deep and swim. Perhaps, when we found her, I could ask her what she'd meant when she said those words. Of course, I had a million questions to ask our mom, like, "Why did you leave? Why did you leave us with Dad? Did you leave *us,* Dad, or *both?*" The list was endless. However, one of my first questions would inevitably be, "What does 'breathe deep and swim' mean?"

Without knowing her intention, I had to apply my own meaning to the phrase. Whether or not it was "correct," there was no way to tell, but I always said this to myself in order to prepare for a challenging task. First, you take a deep breath to build your confidence, as if you are breathing in the world to absorb its strength. Then, you just *go.* You apply yourself to the task and do not stop. You just need to swim. You have to trust in the proverbial water and your own intuition to take you to where you need to go. So, you navigate the watery depths to make your way to your destination. Maybe that's what Van Gogh did every time he took a deep breath. Maybe I was not the only one who ever received this advice. I could've just asked Van Gogh, but I didn't. I liked to think Mom gave me—just *me*—one thing that she didn't give both of us. Even if that wasn't true, it could be my own personal truth.

"What do you remember about Mom?" I asked.

Although I might've been the only one who was told to "breathe deep and swim," I knew that Van Gogh knew more about Mom overall—after all, he had two years more with her than I did.

My brother stared at the road as if he were lost in thought.

"In 100 feet, turn right on Cleveland Avenue and then keep left to continue onto US-41 North," the feminine, robotic voice instructed. Although I was the one who'd plugged our destination into Google Maps, the sound of "her" voice still made me jump.

"I don't know," Van Gogh admitted, gripping the wheel, preparing for the turn. "She looked exactly the way she did in the picture you found. You know, you look a lot like her, actually. Same wavy, light-brown hair and light-blue eyes. I also remember her reading to us each night. I mean, that is until she left. Maybe that's where you get it from. I had never seen her reading any books to herself, but I can't recall a night when she wasn't reading to us. She mostly read us the Golden Books. I'm not sure what happened to them. Anyway, that's pretty much what I remember," Van Gogh concluded, and we took a slight left onto US-41 North.

"Continue on US-41 North for 17 miles," the female voice instructed.

"I don't really remember anything," I admitted. "That picture didn't even trigger a memory."

"Well, you were only a baby in that picture. Plus, Mom left when you were really young. It stands to reason that you don't remember her."

"I wish I did though," I confessed. "It's like a part of us is missing, you know?"

Van Gogh nodded as he concentrated on the road. "Yeah, I get what you mean—but hey, we are headed there now, so she can fill in the missing pieces," he said encouragingly.

"Maybe," I responded, playing with the strings of my N95 mask, wishing that I had more than one for the trip.

I hesitated before asking my next question. I knew my brother wouldn't know the answer, but I was compelled to pose it anyway. I knew it was a question that he must have asked himself. However, I could've been wrong. Sometimes, my brother was easy to read. He didn't believe in keeping secrets, especially from me. He was very upfront with his intentions and beliefs, especially with Dad, which was why they had such a turbulent relationship. However, every once in a while, Van Gogh seemed inaccessible. I didn't know if this was deliberate or instinctual, but there were moments when he was pensive and withdrawn. Although these were rare moments, they felt isolating. I never admitted this to him—that I *needed* him to be accessible and open, that I needed to know that I could rely on someone, and that person would always be him for me. If not Van Gogh, then who? Our mom abandoned us. And to our dad, I was just a nuisance that he didn't really understand. In any case, he was gone now, so it didn't really matter. Whether or not we found our mom, Van Gogh would still be that person because, unlike our parents, he was always there. Even in those rare moments when he seemed to be living inside his head, I knew that eventually he would snap out of it.

"Why do you think Mom left?" I asked.

Van Gogh's knuckles began to turn white as he gripped the wheel a little tighter. Even though we were moving, everything felt very still as I waited for his response. It felt like a good minute before he said anything.

"I wish I knew what to say," he admitted. "I don't know, Wolfgang. I just don't know. She must've had her reasons, but they were always a mystery to me. I'd like to think she left a note, explaining why she chose to leave. It just never made any sense to me. But the fact of the matter is that she left, and if she *did* leave a note, I'm pretty sure it wouldn't have changed anything. She still chose to leave. What's worse is that she chose to leave us with *Dad*." Van Gogh paused to take a deep breath. "But, in spite of all that, she's our only chance."

I nodded, knowing he was right about everything, especially about the fact that Mom not only left us, but that she left us with *Dad*.

Although we both loved Dad, it felt like an obligatory love. This may seem harsh, but I doubted either of us would associate with Dad if he weren't related to us. Yes, he was our father, but to say that he raised us would be a lie. Van Gogh raised me and himself. Our dad provided us with a dwelling, food, and clothing—but that was pretty much it.

Some might argue that that was enough. He was a provider, even if what he provided wasn't consistent. Although he was supposed to provide money for groceries, there were days when our refrigerator was bare. Even though he was supposed to pay the electric and gas bills, there were nights when Van Gogh and I huddled together underneath a blanket, when he held up a flashlight to a book that I was reading so that I could finish the chapter. Since we didn't have a mortgage, we never feared losing our house, but I remember a few times when Dad almost forgot to pay the property taxes.

None of these actions were done out of spite. I just think Dad envisioned a life for himself where his wife took care of these tasks. I would've never said this to him, but I firmly believed that he wasn't prepared to be a responsible adult, let alone a single father to two sons. But even though *I* would never criticize Dad to his face, Van Gogh was much more confrontational and open about his feelings. In fact, my brother had even told Dad that he was an unfit father.

It happened pretty recently after we first suspected Dad had COVID-19. His cough was so dry and persistent, we couldn't help but wonder if it was from our dad's irrational insistence on smoking one pack of cigarettes a day, or from something else. However, when his frequent coughing fits left him lightheaded and out of breath, Van Gogh and I began to suspect that he had the coronavirus.

Despite our suspicions, Dad had continued to go to his job at the construction site—until he was too tired to move, at least. At that point, Van Gogh called in sick for him. That was only a couple of days ago.

Dad never admitted that he was sick. Even before he got sick, he never wore a mask or socially distanced himself from others. Once it became impossible for Dad to take care of himself, my brother ensured he remained in his bedroom. It became a makeshift hospital room, without a ventilator or any monitoring system. It was the best we could do since neither of us could carry him to the car, and any time we even attempted to call 911, Dad forced all his energy into yelling at us, screaming to get off the phone. By the time he could no longer scream—or speak, for that matter—he was too far gone. Near the end, Van Gogh and I knew there was no point in taking him to the hospital.

However, before this point, Van Gogh had one final confrontation with our dad. It was essentially the last conversation they ever had.

"Face it, you have COVID-19!" Van Gogh had exclaimed as Dad doubled over from his latest coughing fit. "You need to go to the hospital."

Dad cleared his throat and leaned against the wall, trying to balance himself.

"Look, Van, it's just a damn cough," Dad asserted, wiping the beads of sweat forming on his brow. "Mind your own business."

"Mind my own business! Are you kidding me?" Van Gogh had screamed, clenching his fists while taking a step away from our dad, trying to keep his distance. "This is *my business!* We"—Van Gogh pointed to him and me—"are in this house with you! You are putting us in danger!"

"You don't know what—" Dad was cut off by another coughing fit. He pressed his palm against the wall as he coughed into his fist, which barely covered his mouth. I slid deeper into the couch and raised the book I was reading up to my face, as though I could shield myself from his illness through the sheer force of literature.

"I don't know *what*, Dad? I don't know that you can't get out a damn sentence because you are coughing up a lung!" Van Gogh raked his fingers through his hair as he scowled out our dad, who continued to cough. "I don't know that you are endangering the guys on the site! I don't know that you are endangering everyone in that damn bar who refuses to wear a mask! What don't I understand, Dad?!"

After his coughing fit, Dad stared directly into Van Gogh's matching lily-pad-green eyes. They were both so piercing, and so stubborn—firmly believing in their own opinions, deeming the other one as an adversary.

But maybe that was appropriate. These fights had come to define their relationship. If they weren't fighting, they weren't interacting. They merely coexisted in this house; their relationship was marred by their refusal to try to understand one another.

Dad didn't understand me either, but unlike Van Gogh, I never confronted him about his beliefs or conjectures. I just stayed out of his way, resigned to the fact that he would never try to understand me, so why bother to fight with him? Why waste my energy? While this attitude came naturally to me, Van Gogh had a hard time letting anything go. Unlike me, he was a fighter, but so was Dad.

When you put two fighters in a ring and do not expect a fight to break out, you are just a fool.

"You don't know *anything*!" Dad had growled. "Just stay out of it."

"Unbelievable! *Stay out of it*!" Van Gogh's veins were prominently bulging from his neck as he continued. "You go on about how COVID-19 is *nothing* and talk about how '*fake news*' sensationalizes this pandemic! But even when you catch it, you don't believe in it! To you, it's none of my business, but it *is* my damn business because you can give it to me–to Wolfgang! Don't you care? Don't you give a damn about yourself, about us?"

To that, Dad said nothing. He just continued to look Van Gogh straight in the eyes. I don't know what he was trying to accomplish in doing so, but Van Gogh played the game and stared back. I don't even know if he was waiting for an answer to his question, but Dad's silence said it all.

"You know what?" Van Gogh scoffed, "You don't. I mean, how could you? You've never been a damn father. You're only related to us biologically, but you don't have it in you to be a father."

By this time, Dad was fuming. His face was as purplish red as a beet, which was caused by a mixture of coughing and rage.

"Get out," Dad had growled.

Before he could say anything else, Van Gogh picked up his sketchpad and pencils from the coffee table and marched out of the house. As the door slammed shut, a flood of regret had poured over me. *Why didn't I go with you, Van Gogh? What if you don't return? Why didn't I follow you?*

As I sat next to Van Gogh in the car now—looking down at Google Maps, watching us inch closer and closer to New York—I knew I wouldn't make the same mistake again. I knew I would follow Van Gogh wherever he led. It was the only way that we could survive.

THREE

CHOICES

The coffin was gray, which seemed impossible because coffins were usually brown or black. However, I was not an expert. Maybe the color of this coffin was a deliberate choice. We all make certain choices in our lives that lead to our particular fates. I accepted this reality, but what I could never really grasp was how a seemingly minute move or thought had the possibility to determine your fate. When you sense a choice is life changing, then you are more prepared to expect the change, even if you are not prepared to accept it.

I felt as if I was moving through sludge as I inched closer to the coffin. It seemed to stand alone in a blurry room. I hadn't been to an optometrist in a while so maybe my peripheral vision was going, but this didn't make sense, as it was fine before… before what, exactly? How did I even get here?

My feet didn't give me enough time to consider how I wound up facing a coffin, because I kept moving forward, as though compelled by some invisible force. The coffin seemed to be lost, yet still blaringly visible, in a milky fog.

I could feel my pulse accelerating, setting my pace as I began to move more quickly. The rapidity of my heartbeat was unbearable. When would it stop? Would my heart pound so fast it would blow a fuse? That's not even possible, but what would happen if it refused to stop? So many unsuspecting people say that they are too young, or too healthy to have a heart attack, to get sick—however, if this year of my life has taught me anything, it's that the "impossible" doesn't exist. Anything is possible under the right circumstances.

I was only inches away from the coffin when my feet suddenly stopped. It felt as if they were glued to the floor, as my body slightly bent forward to peer into the coffin. But it was closed.

"Open it," a voice commanded. The voice was familiar but it seemed disembodied. It had a firm tenor that I just couldn't place.

My hands were like a puppet's as they instinctively followed the command. Ironically, my heart's rhythm began to slow as I gingerly lifted the lid.

I tried to avert my gaze, but my head would not move and my eyelids would not close. My entire body and my brain were at odds as I pushed the lid of the coffin up.

As I looked down at the dark-brown hair, and glassy, porcelain-like lily-pad-green eyes, I fought to scream, but my lips pressed into one another, muffling the screams echoing in my head. His dark-charcoal suit was too grown-up, too formal for his youthful face.

"Say goodbye to your brother," the voice commanded, as the coffin slammed shut.

"No!" I screamed, jolting upright from the car seat, feeling the pressure of the seat belt pushing me back into place.

"Hey, are you okay?" Van Gogh asked, pulling into a lot.

"What? What happened?" I asked, looking up into the burgeoning reddish-orange skyline.

"You were asleep," Van Gogh informed me, easing the car into park. "I didn't want to wake you. You were out for a few hours."

It took my eyes a minute to adjust to the daylight. Before I could ask Van Gogh where we were, I noticed the bright blue and yellow gas station sign hanging prominently overhead.

I was amazed by Van Gogh's stamina. How he was able to drive for hours, I would never know—but Van Gogh never needed a lot of sleep. I guess you could argue that we were most productive at night. I would read by flashlight while Van Gogh would turn on a lamp light to draw or paint either in the living room or in our bedroom.

Our dad had clearly minded, but he didn't seem to mind *when* we were drawing or reading; it was the very *act* that annoyed him. That was why I chose to read and Van Gogh chose to draw or paint at night—that was usually when we could avoid Dad's judgmental gaze. While Van Gogh always seemed up for a fight with Dad, he knew the confrontations bothered me. However, sometimes these battles were unavoidable, like their last argument. As Van Gogh would say, "Sometimes you just need to upend the table. Not out of spite, but out of necessity. You can't let that anger boil inside you. It's bound to come out at some point."

We'd both known Dad's resentment toward Mom was still simmering within him. I wouldn't be surprised if his last thoughts were focused on his hatred for her. Or perhaps he was just looking up at the ceiling, believing that his symptoms were a result of drinking too much beer. Anything is possible. However, something told me that he was definitely not thinking about us—that is, unless he was wishing that we were more like "his sons."

When I was younger, whenever our dad told us to act more like "his sons," I couldn't help but get entangled in the paradoxical notion of that statement. We did not need our birth certificates to confirm that we were biologically his sons, and as far as we knew, he did not have any other children, so if we were, indeed, his actual sons, then how were we not acting like his sons?

When I first heard him say that, I made the mistake of asking him what he meant.

"Don't talk back!" he'd snarled.

"How am I talking back?" I asked, not understanding what that statement meant until Van Gogh explained it to me.

"You're doing it now! Just go to your room," Dad had said as he eased onto the couch and searched for the remote control.

I'd walked into our room—which even seven years ago still looked exactly the same, except the bookcase held fewer books, and Van Gogh only had a sketch pad and colored pencils.

Van Gogh had been sitting on his bed, gazing out the window as he held his sketch pad in one hand and a green pencil in the other. He seemed lost in the scenery, as if he'd forgotten what he was doing in mid-action. He tended to do this from time to time. I never knew exactly what he was thinking about, but he just seemed to be looking at some indiscriminate scene or item that did not require him to focus his stare. It was as if he needed to look at the whole span of scenery, whatever that scenery may be, instead of one particular focal point.

"Van Gogh?" I'd asked. "What does Dad mean when he says that we're not like his sons? It doesn't really make sense because we *are* his sons. I don't understand."

Van Gogh shook his head at my naivety and turned to face me. Even at nine years old, Van Gogh furrowed his brow when he was trying to think of how to articulate his thoughts in a way that would make sense to me.

"What he means is that he wishes that we were different," he'd explained.

"Different how?"

"You know, more like him," Van Gogh stated, placing his unfinished drawing and pencil on his bed. "I mean, we don't have a lot in common. That bothers him."

Even as a child, Van Gogh had more insight into our dad than I ever could. Seven years later, I may have understood the meaning of some of our dad's actions and choices, but I could rarely empathize with him. It was for this reason that we were never close. Maybe that's why I didn't cry when I'd found him. I wouldn't describe myself as "tough" or even brave. Crying never bothered me. However, when I'd found my dad's body, although I was sickened by his appearance, I didn't feel a sense of emotional loss, but rather the loss of life in our living space. It was like we were just people cohabiting in the same house, rather than father and son. I knew why I wasn't tethered to him, and yet I couldn't help but question what my apathy conveyed about me.

Before Van Gogh could step out of the car to put gas in the tank, I turned to him. "Did you cry at all?"

He paused, pulling the ajar car door back shut.

"You mean about Dad." It seemed like this should have been a question, but he seemed to be stating an understanding. Van Gogh usually was able to intuit what I was thinking.

"Yeah, did you cry? I mean, I know you didn't hysterically cry, but did your eyes fill up, or did you even feel a bit of sadness?"

Van Gogh stared at some indiscriminate scene again with his furrowed brow before responding.

"No." His monosyllabic response spoke volumes. I wasn't surprised that he didn't mourn Dad, either. Although he passionately fought with Dad, it wasn't out of love, but rather out of stubbornness, self-assertion, and protectiveness. I'd once heard love and hate compared to the concept of yin and yang. These strong emotions are polar opposites but are simultaneously and fervently tied together. You need a bit of love to hate and vice versa. However, this was not the case with Dad. Also, it could be argued that Van Gogh hated our father, but this hatred had been temporary. It was the hate you feel when you see a stranger committing injustice, or when you hear somebody make a racist slur. However, it wasn't the hate you feel when you know that a loved one has betrayed you. I think our dad's lack of love for us soured any emotional connection we once had for him. This is why we did not—and would never—mourn him.

Before I could say anything more, Van Gogh reached over the driver's side seat to grab his backpack. He fished around until he found the wad of cash. He gingerly slipped a few twenties out of the wad and handed me a bill.

"While I fill up, go into the store and grab us some snacks," Van Gogh said, placing a hand on my shoulder before getting out of the car.

The store was just a typical gas station convenience store, but somehow it felt roomier, almost as if it were a makeshift 7-Eleven without the ubiquitous Slurpee machine. As I navigated the store—which was almost completely devoid of people, except for myself, the cashier, and someone in the back that I really couldn't see—I picked out a few essentials: a couple extra masks, two bottles of water, a few bags of mixed nuts and trail mix, and some coffee cakes.

As I carried the bundle in my arms, I regretted not grabbing a basket. Luckily, there was no line at the counter. I slowly walked up to the "six feet apart" sticker, and once waved over by the cashier, I placed my items in front of the plexiglass barrier.

"My brother should be coming in to pay you for the gas," I said as the cashier rang up the items. He muttered something about that being fine as he placed the items into a paper bag.

Before he could announce my total, I heard a muffled, "Hands up!" to the right of me.

I hesitated to move, thinking that I must have misunderstood what I heard, but when I saw the cashier's face turn a sickening white and his dark eyes widen as he slowly raised his arms up in the air, I mirrored his action.

I was tempted to turn toward the harsh, muffled voice barking orders at the cashier, but I resisted the temptation when I heard, "Give me all the money in the cash register!"

If I did not see the imposing, jet-black handgun poised at the cashier out of the corner of my eye, I would've thought that this was some elaborate joke. How much can a gas station cash register really hold?

I stared through the plexiglass shield, knowing that if the robber pulled the trigger, the plexiglass would not hold. The cashier's shaky hands fumbled on the keys of the cash register, making several attempts to open it. Finally, the ding of the register sounded, signaling that he was successful. He anxiously pulled out bills and coins, placing them to the side.

"Count 'em!" The robber barked, readjusting his aim.

I could feel my heart beating throughout my body as I concentrated on keeping both of my arms extended above my head.

"Keep 'em up!" The robber announced. I couldn't help but slightly turn my head to look in his direction. His face was covered by a black ski mask, which did not match his blue jeans and camouflage T-shirt. His piercing, bloodshot brown eyes seemed to stare directly into mine, but only for a moment until his gaze shifted from side to side. I understood why the cashier was anxious, but this guy had all the power—so why did he appear cagey, almost desperate?

"Hurry up!" he barked at the cashier once again, as the cashier nervously placed the bills in piles of twenties, tens, fives, and singles.

"Yes, sir," the cashier stammered as he began to collect the piles.

I would have looked around the store to see if anyone was hiding in the corner, calling for help, but the robber was homed in on me, almost as if he suspected that I would try to call for help. It was at that moment that I realized that I left my cell phone in the car. I had needed to turn it off in order to save the battery life. I closed my eyes, realizing my stupidity, wishing that I were just having another horrific nightmare that I would awaken from any second.

"Don't move," a voice commanded.

For a moment, I thought the robber was addressing me, but before I could open my mouth to tell him I wasn't moving, I heard, "Who the hell are you?"

"Put the gun down," I heard a familiar voice command. I mustered up all the courage I had to turn around to see Van Gogh aiming a shotgun at the robber's head.

Van Gogh's right index finger rested on the silver trigger while he gripped the fore-end of the gun with his left. He had the stock to his cheek with the butt wedged into his shoulder pocket. He was standing up straighter than usual, with his knees slightly bent, just like our dad taught him to do. Although Van Gogh and I had nothing in common with our dad, when we were younger, he'd made several attempts to share his interests with us. He'd taught us how to fish, play darts, build my old bookcase, and how to hunt. But unlike my brother, I could never bring myself to hold a gun, let alone shoot one.

Before the robber could respond, Van Gogh said, "I already called the cops. They will be here any second. Get the hell out of here while you still can."

Van Gogh's stare was laser focused, as if he were trying to dig into the thief's eyes from a distance.

"Fuck off, kid!" the robber exclaimed, turning the gun toward me. "Or this one will get shot."

I tried to swallow, but my throat and mouth were suddenly as dry as the Sahara.

Without missing a beat, Van Gogh said, "Before you even think of pulling your trigger, I'll blow a hole through you so large that your grandchildren will feel it."

As Van Gogh finished his sentence, we all heard the faint sounds of police sirens growing louder. At that moment, the robber let out a few expletives, dropped both arms, and ran out the back—leaving the stacks of money behind, which had finally been pulled together.

Van Gogh stared at the spot where the robber had stood as he lowered the shotgun. Before either the cashier or I could say anything, Van Gogh threw thirty dollars on the counter and said, "Thanks for the gas." He quickly ran toward the store's exit, checking to make sure neither the robber nor the cops could see us.

I ran so closely behind him, I felt almost like his shadow.

"It's clear. Run to the car," he commanded as we slipped out and jetted to our car.

Both of us ducking, we ran as quickly as possible to the Pontiac. I slipped in the passenger's side seat, while Van Gogh ran to the back of the car. I turned to see the trunk of the car pop open, and then heard it quickly slam shut. As the sirens grew louder, he slipped into the driver's side and put the key in the ignition.

He peeled out of the gas station so fast, I didn't have a moment to tell him to slow down, otherwise the cops may mistake us for the robber. But as we turned down a side street and then another, I heard the sirens grow a little fainter, and with that, my heartbeat slowed down to a rhythmic march.

I closed my eyes, feeling the surge of adrenaline running through me. I had this urge to jump out of the car and keep running, as though I could outrun a car. But hearing my brother's voice brought me back to reality.

"Are you okay?" he asked, pulling over to the side of the road. "I don't think we're being followed." He turned his head around, scanning the perimeter, almost as if expecting the police to be hiding, waiting to pounce.

"Yeah." I coughed. "I'm okay," I said, pulling off my mask and placing it beside me.

After a few seconds of silence, I asked, "How?" I tried to catch my breath. Under normal circumstances, I could run for long distances without needing to catch my breath, but that short run to the car had felt like it was ten miles long. "How did you know?"

Without missing a beat, Van Gogh simply stated, "That store has large windows. Anyone who was filling up could have seen what was going on. I just happened to be one of the only people outside, so I had to do something."

Van Gogh picked up my phone. "I think it still has some juice. Can you turn it back on?"

I focused on steadying my arm as I took it from him and plugged in my pin. Once I heard the robotic voice of the GPS woman direct us, I placed the phone beside me.

Nodding at the sound of the directions, Van Gogh put the car into drive and pressed his foot onto the accelerator.

"Van Gogh, why do you have Dad's shotgun?" I tried to recall if he'd taken this with him when we left our house, but I could only picture him with his backpack and our dad's car keys.

"Dad always forgot to bring in his shotgun. Don't you remember how many times he would riffle through the house, cursing because he couldn't remember where he left it, only to realize he forgot it in the trunk?"

"We could have been killed," I asserted, the image of the robber aiming his handgun directly at me seared into my mind. Van Gogh shook his head in response, as though trying to use his head to shake the thought out of my mind. "No," he said firmly. "That man wouldn't have killed either of us." He said this statement with such certainty and defiance that it was unbelievable. Van Gogh had always been confident, but how could he be so sure that we wouldn't have died in that gas station convenience store?

"I know this," he continued, "because that guy had no idea what he was doing."

"How do you know?"

"Easy," he said, turning back onto the highway. "His safety was on the whole time. That, and I would never let anything bad happen to you."

Even though I knew logically Van Gogh could never promise nothing bad would happen to me, his sense of assurance and confidence was comforting. Although this might have been irrational, just knowing that he believed he could prevent anything bad from happening to me was all I needed to feel safe.

FOUR

DISCOVERY

Sometimes, in the battle of willpower, the body defeats the mind. For this reason, Van Gogh was forced to pull over to the side of the road. Although it was midmorning, I could see my brother constantly shaking his head, trying to focus.

I didn't really need to persuade him to pull over. I simply asked if we could just take a moment to rest, and then he just took the next exit and found a little parking lot.

Once we pulled into the space and Van Gogh turned off the engine, he slumped into the driver's seat and closed his eyes. He muttered something about waking him up in a few minutes, but I didn't know why we were in such a rush. I mean, the police were not following us, and how likely was it that our dad's body would be discovered within the next few hours?

I took this opportunity to reread one of my books, but when I searched through my backpack, the first book I pulled out was one that I had never read before: *Madame Bovary* by Gustave Flaubert. I couldn't help but wonder why our dad had two books tucked in the back of the closet, especially one that, according to the translator's introduction, was published in France in 1857. It was one thing if he'd had an angler magazine or Trump paraphernalia in the back of the closet, but a nineteenth-century French novel? That made no sense.

When I felt the spine, I could feel the deep-seated cracks, suggesting the book had been read and reread several times. It wasn't until I opened the book that I realized this book definitely did *not* belong to my dad. The margins of the pages were covered in annotations. The penmanship was written in a neat, curvy script. As I scanned the pages, I noticed that, while some of the annotations were written in pencil, others were written in either black or blue pen, creating the illusion that multiple people had written in this book—but the penmanship was identical.

After flipping through the entire book, I noticed that a few passages and sentences were highlighted, especially toward the beginning. The one that stood out was not only highlighted, but the reader had chosen to write an annotation next to it. Next to the line, "But in her eagerness for a change, or perhaps overstimulated by this man's presence, she easily persuaded herself that love, that marvelous thing which had hitherto been like a great rosy-plumaged bird soaring in the splendors of poetic skies, was at last within her grasp," the reader simply wrote, "*Ben.*" Ben? As in, Ben *Thomas*? Ben was a common name, but how likely was it that my dad's name was written inside of a book that was in the back of his closet?

That was when it occurred to me that this was my mom's book. Although, for me, this sentence was taken completely out of context, it was pretty obvious that the sentence reminded Mom of Dad. According to the sentence, she—maybe Madame Bovary?—had persuaded herself that she was in love with a man because she was seeking a change. Was it possible that she'd highlighted the passage because this situation reflected her own? Maybe when reality hit her, she realized she didn't genuinely love Dad, but rather wanted to love him in order to escape from something.

Before I could jump to any more conclusions, I flipped the book back to the first page, and I began to read.

I must have been reading for hours before I heard my brother stir and ask, "What time is it?"

I took a quick glance at my phone. "1:15," I stated, almost in the form of a question. Had I really been reading for that long?

Van Gogh seemed to share my surprise as he bolted upright and rammed the key into the ignition.

"You should have woken me up earlier!" he exclaimed.

"Van Gogh, wait," I said before he could shift into reverse. "Why are we in such a rush? No one is after us."

"Yeah, not now, but they will be. We can't risk it. We have to go."

Maybe it was from reading our mom's annotations, or maybe I just needed some time to process the situation, but I realized that he'd overlooked something.

"Wait, Van Gogh, you said that we would be placed in foster care if Dad's body was discovered, right?" I said. Van Gogh nodded. "Okay, but they would try to locate our next of kin, right? I mean, wouldn't they contact Mom? Wouldn't that be their first move? She is our next of kin."

Van Gogh took his right hand off of the gear shift and turned off the engine.

"Maybe, but there's something you're not considering." He took a deep breath before continuing his explanation. "Look, I think you're right. Yes, they would probably try to track Mom down. And yes, they would probably notify her about Dad's death . . . but it's not that simple." My brother turned to face me. His lily-pad-green eyes seemed lighter, more thoughtful. "What happens if she is contacted, but she still doesn't want us?"

I opened my mouth to respond, but I had no words. I hadn't even considered the possibility of Mom refusing to take us in. The only response I had was a question that I did not want to know the answer to. But I had to ask it anyway.

"If that's the case, then why are we trying to find her?"

Van Gogh looked down at *Madame Bovary*, almost as if he were looking to our mom's old book for answers.

"It's a lot easier to reject someone who you don't really know. I mean, imagine a stranger calling her and asking, 'Will you care for your sons who you haven't seen in over a decade?' Maybe she could refuse over the phone because we are just names. We are just 'wards of the state,' but if we looked her in the eye and explained the situation, if she saw us in person … well, it's a lot harder to reject someone when they are right in front of you."

I couldn't argue with his point. However, I couldn't help but ask the question that I knew was on both of our minds. "What if she still says no? What then?"

Van Gogh took another deep breath and seemed to hold it in for a beat before exhaling. "I don't know, but we at least have to try. It's our only shot." And then he put the key back into the ignition and pulled out of the spot.

I looked down at *Madame Bovary* and hoped that my brother was right. If only we knew more about our mom, then maybe we could predict how she would respond when she saw us—*if* she saw us. We didn't really have an address; we just knew where she'd lived before she married Dad. It was very likely that she had run away to another state since, potentially another country. I mean, we could hire a private investigator to track her down, but at this point, it was too late. If we were discovered, we would be placed in foster care before we could even track down a private investigator.

Our chances of success were very slim. I once heard that, when rolling dice, you have one in six chances of rolling your desired number. As we drove toward New York, we had a one in six shot of our mom accepting the two sons, her family, that she ran away from well over a decade ago.

"Are you hungry?" Van Gogh asked, pulling into a diner's parking lot.

I felt the car ease to a stop and heard the distinct jingle of the car keys as Van Gogh shoved them into his pocket. Although this was not a line that our mom had highlighted, the thought did cross my mind that, similar to Emma Bovary, maybe she was inaccessible. Even though she wasn't a provincial doctor's wife in nineteenth-century France, maybe, like Madame Bovary, she sought more out of life. It's entirely possible that to her, we were like her daughter, Berthe—a burden that she was left with. That is, until she found a way to escape.

"You coming?" Van Gogh asked, pulling on his mask.

I nodded as I exchanged the book for my N95 mask and got out of the car.

The diner was a vinyl salmon-pink and lime-green color. If going to diners on a regular basis had taught me anything, it was that the food would look just as funky and artificial.

Van Gogh nodded toward a booth, where we adjusted into the uncomfortable seats. Before I could pick up a menu, a waitress, whose outfit matched the colors of the walls and booth, came by with a pad and pencil.

"What will you have?" she asked distractedly, looking over at the flat-screen TV perched over the counter. Pencil poised over her pad, she scribbled down our order of coffee and grilled cheese sandwiches with tomato soup.

"Coming up," she said as she walked away, eyes fixed on the news station.

I shrugged as I pushed the menu to the side and looked out the window at our Pontiac.

"This needs to be our last stop for a while," Van Gogh said, pulling out his phone. "At this rate, we're definitely going to have to drive at night."

I hesitated to push back, feeling his determination emanating off of him like a soft but distinct glow.

"Do you want me to drive?" I offered.

Van Gogh raised one eyebrow and smirked as he shook his head.

"Wolfgang, you've never driven a car in your life, and you are choosing to drive now? On major highways?"

I straightened up, as if my posture would prove my worth. "Why not? You don't even have a license and you are driving."

"Yeah, but I have driven before, plenty of times, especially when Dad was too drunk to drive," he said. "Plus, you've never offered to drive, why now?"

As I stared at the dark circles forming under his eyes, I hesitated to explain why.

"Coffee," the waitress barked, magically appearing at our table with two steaming mugs. "Your meal is coming up," she announced before she drifted off to another table.

I slowly sipped the bitter, acidic coffee, regretting not asking for cream. Van Gogh practically chugged his as he placed the empty mug on the table and looked out the window at yet another indiscriminate point.

As we waited for our meal, I couldn't help but wonder if my brother was right about Mom. If she saw us, *would* she be more likely to accept us? Why should seeing us make a difference? In a sense, Van Gogh *was* right—it was by far a lot harder to reject someone in person than it would be over the phone or online. However, there were individuals who could just as easily say no to someone when they saw them face-to-face. I didn't know enough about Mom to say that she wouldn't react like that, but then again, I couldn't say that she would. I only knew that if Van Gogh believed this was our only choice, I would have to trust his judgment, even if I had my doubts.

"Two grilled cheese sandwiches and two tomato soups," the waitress announced, once again appearing out of nowhere. This time, she almost made me jump as she placed our bowls and plates in front of us. Once again, she turned toward the TV, muttering something about letting her know when we needed the check.

As I bit into the grilled cheese—which surprisingly wasn't half bad—I turned toward the TV screen to see what exactly was so fascinating. That is when I saw the distinct gray hair that seemed so fitting for his name— Grayson Tanner, our dad's foreman. I immediately recognized the one-story, pale-green house in the background.

I took another bite of my grilled cheese sandwich, but the pieces went down like sandpaper. I placed the sandwich back on the plate as I leaned out of the booth, trying to listen to my dad's boss—well, *former* boss.

"So, you say you just found him in his home?" the reporter asked, standing a sizable distance from Grayson, both of whom were wearing thin blue medical masks.

Grayson crossed his arms over his typical blue flannel shirt and matching coat as he nodded. This was how he would be etched in my memory—a nodding blue flannel shirt in front of our one-story, pale-green house.

"Yeah, he hadn't come to work in quite a while, so I came down to personally check in when I found the front door unlocked."

I squeezed my eyes shut. *I knew we'd forgotten to do something before we left.*

"I don't know what, but something told me to walk into his house," Grayson continued. "And that's when I found him in his bed."

The reporter nodded and pivoted toward the camera. "Thank you, Mr. Tanner. Medical examiners were able to determine that Benjamin Thomas died from COVID-19. This is one of the many COVID-19 losses we have experienced this month as the numbers continue to rise. Benjamin Thomas, father of two, was forty-four years old. Authorities have not been able to locate his sons, but they haven't been reported missing yet."

As the reporter continued speaking, my attention drifted back to my sandwich, which now looked foreign to me. I looked up to see Van Gogh's head turned toward the TV, his stare growing more intense as he listened to the reporter continue.

Even after the report transitioned to another story, my brother's eyes remained fixed on the TV screen. It took me saying his name a few times for him to finally snap out of his trance. He shook his head and placed his unfinished grilled cheese sandwich on his plate. Running his fingers through his dark-brown hair, he looked down at his untouched bowl of soup.

"Van Gogh?" No response. I cleared my throat. "Van Gogh. What are we going to do?" Once again, I was looking to my brother for guidance.

"Check!" Van Gogh requested to no one in particular, but as if expecting his call, the waitress floated over and placed the check between our barely eaten sandwiches. "We're leaving," Van Gogh announced as he pulled his mask on and placed a few bills on the table. "We can't stay here."

At his command, I grabbed my mask and hurried to catch up to my brother, who seemed to sprint out the door. I barely got in the car before he was revving the engine and pulling out of the lot.

We drove in silence for what felt like an hour. The GPS system kept recalculating as Van Gogh ignored its guidance. I finally asked if I should turn it off, but Van Gogh didn't nod or shake his head; his gaze was firmly on the road in front of him.

"Van Gogh? I... I'm going to turn it off," I said, biting back asking the questions on the tip of my tongue. *Where are we going? What are we going to do next? What is the plan, Van Gogh?* I desperately wanted to know, and I think he knew that. I think he also knew that it was only a matter of time before I couldn't prevent myself from asking those questions. I only hoped that Van Gogh had answers.

One or two hours passed in deafening silence. I longed to continue reading *Madame Bovary*, not because the book interested me, but merely to have more insight into our mom—if the book would offer that. Her annotations seemed pointed and purposeful, but I still didn't have a sense of who she is *was*—or who she potentially could still be. But I just couldn't continue without knowing the plan. *Where are we going? What are we going to do next? What is the plan, Van Gogh?*

As predicted, I couldn't help myself.

Van Gogh's brow furrowed as he turned over my questions in his mind.

"We still have to find her," Van Gogh began to explain, his steady gaze on the road ahead, which was littered with other moving cars heading toward some unknown destination. "But we need to make a detour."

"Wait—why? Where?" I asked in quick succession.

"*Why?* Wolfgang, it's only a matter of time before the police or child protective services—probably *both*—come looking for us. You know what will happen if they catch us. We just can't take that chance."

"How will they know where we are? I mean, it's not like we were ever implanted with tracking devices," I offered.

"No, but they can trace our phones, and guess whose car we are driving?"

Van Gogh was right. It was only a matter of time before they found us. It was possible that child protective services and the police wouldn't waste all of that energy trying to track us down, but as Van Gogh noted, we just couldn't take that chance.

"Okay, then what's the plan?"

Van Gogh signaled to the right and got off at the next exit. As we headed down the exit ramp, Van Gogh opened both car windows and chucked his cell phone out of the speeding car.

"Your turn," he said simply.

Without hesitation, I followed suit and watched my cell phone smash into the pavement, leaving a shattered, splintery metallic mess on the side of who-knows-what road.

FIVE

BECOMING UNTRACEABLE

Without a GPS system making commands, I had no idea where we were going, or why Van Gogh was continuing to drive in some unknown direction. He and Dad had always boasted about their "amazing sense of direction," but how can you have a "sense of direction" when you're driving in the middle of nowhere?

At least if we were still on the highway, we could use the exit signs as some sort of guide, but now we were gliding down street after side street with no end in sight. Even when driving down a dead end, Van Gogh merely made a U-turn and headed down a different street.

It was pointless to ask where we were going again because every time I posed the question, Van Gogh would merely say, "We'll know when we get there."

Although driving in a directionless direction put me ill at ease, I knew there was no turning back. *Why did you throw out your phone?* I kept asking myself, combatting my twinge of regret with my loyalty to Van Gogh. *You did it because it was a part of the plan. You could've been caught.*

But then my own personal devil's advocate retorted, *What plan? There is no plan. He is just telling you vague bits and pieces. How can you follow a non-plan plan?*

A rebuttal: *He'll figure it out, you just have to have patience. You just have to have faith. Just breathe deep and swim. It will all work out.*

And there it was, from my own subconscious—"breathe deep and swim." I just had to go with it; I had to rebel against every urge to find a sense of certainty and security because we were living within an uncertain time, on a personal and global scale.

Closing my eyes, I took a deep breath and held it for a moment, trying to swim in the darkness I saw before me. I didn't know how long I sat with my eyes closed, but once I finally opened them, I didn't even look at the endless, unknown street signs ahead. Instead, I picked up *Madame Bovary* once again and began to read.

"We're here," I heard Van Gogh say before I felt him ease the car into park. Based on the sizable dent I'd made in the book, we must have been driving around for a few hours. As I opened the car door, I could feel that the temperature had dropped a few degrees and that the whispers of dusk were lapping at the sky.

"Grab everything you want to take with you," my brother commanded, pushing the driver's seat forward and grabbing his backpack.

Biting back my questions, I reached for my backpack and pulled on my N95 mask. I instinctively felt the seat for my cell phone before remembering I threw it away. Feeling confident that I had everything with me, I shoved *Madame Bovary* into my backpack before getting out of the car.

Standing beside the car, I could not believe the view. Microscopic flecks of salt trickled into the ocean breeze as I looked out onto the foamy waves. The tan, smooth, sandy beach expanded beyond measurement and was well within walking distance. I eased my backpack onto my shoulders, watching the aquamarine waves lap at the vulnerable sandy ground.

I looked toward Van Gogh, who calmly looked out over the Atlantic Ocean. A memory of him, Dad, Uncle Earl, and me sitting on the beach began to form. We may not have been on this particular beach, but the lapping waves and scent of salt were unforgettable. It had been my first time facing an ocean, let alone such an expansive and pervasive one.

I didn't recall the drive, or where we'd parked, but I did remember the gentle, pliable sand giving way to my weight. How it molded to my form had left such an imprint on me. I was fascinated by the disintegration of the ground that oddly, but inevitably, firmly held us up. Before arriving at the beach, I'd read about the dangers of the ironically named "quicksand," and how stepping into that sand could mean certain death. Although I didn't remember my exact age, I did remember being relieved that the sand we stepped on was neither quick nor slow, just present and stable.

Uncle Earl and Dad had set up two beach chairs next to their cooler, which was packed with ice, beer, and sandwiches. I remember my brother sitting on a beach towel—which was really just one of our bath towels—while looking out at the horizon, his sketchpad in one hand and a blue pencil in the other. The rest of his colored pencils were neatly tucked in their box, waiting to be used to replicate the view. Van Gogh swiftly tilted the pencil on its side and pressed the side of the tip into the paper, creating a series of fading, thick blue lines. As he drew, I sat beside him, arm against arm, as he made room for me beside him, continuing to draw.

I'd pulled a book from my backpack, but I couldn't recall the title because as soon as I'd pulled it out, Dad called over, "Who brings a book to the beach?" Van Gogh and I both turned in his direction as he continued. "Act like normal kids and go into the ocean," he commanded, laughing while taking another sip of beer.

Without opening the book, I placed it back in my backpack and began to get up from the blanket—that is, until I felt a firm yet gentle grip on my arm holding me in place.

"Hey, stay here a second," Van Gogh said, pulling his legs to him, resting his sketchpad onto his thighs, which he fashioned into a makeshift easel. Continuing to look out at the horizon, he added, "Don't let anyone— especially him—tell you who to be or what to do. If you want to read, then read. It doesn't mean you're not normal."

I looked down at my closed backpack, taking in Van Gogh's words. Although we were both very young, he'd never seemed naive. He always seemed to have a deeper understanding of the world, and more insight into people than I did. Maybe it was because he consistently studied everything, trying to replicate it in his drawings, that made him understand. Perhaps this was why he was able to understand our dad—but understanding didn't translate to empathy.

"I don't know," I'd said, shrugging. "I mean, we *are* at the beach. Maybe the right thing to do would be to go into the water."

"In this case, there is no such thing as 'right' or 'wrong.' You need to do what you want to do. Trust your instincts, Wolfgang. If you want to go into the water, then let's go for it—but we'll only go when you want to, not because someone told you that it is not 'normal' to *not* go in. Got it?"

I nodded. Van Gogh placed a hand on my shoulder while continuing to draw the horizon with the other. We must've stayed that way for a while before I decided to head into the ocean's salty body.

"Hey, help me with this toolbox," my brother called from behind the car.

Pulling myself out of my reverie, I walked to the back of the car to find the trunk popped open and Van Gogh riffling through our dad's rusted red toolbox. The box was punctuated with indentations from years of being flung back and forth in the trunk, inevitably smacking into the shotgun that had lain beside it.

I instinctively looked around to see if anyone could see the shotgun clearly displayed within the trunk, but the area was practically barren. I flashed back to Van Gogh, steadily aiming the gun at the thief. His eyes had been so confident and fixed. Although he'd had experience using the gun, I knew he'd never shot a living creature before. When Dad would get angry at my brother's alleged "poor aim," Van Gogh would simply shrug off the criticism. We both knew he was purposely aiming slightly to the left or right of his target, far enough away to cause the animal to scatter or fly when it heard the deafening boom of the gun.

Despite the fact that Van Gogh knew how to use the gun, I still couldn't believe that he'd been able to muster up the bravery to aim it at a human being—thief or not. I guess in dire situations, you're able to do the impossible, or at least what you once thought was impossible. Under the right circumstances, perhaps we really were capable of anything.

"Hmm…he must have it in here," Van Gogh said, pulling out a hammer and wrench, placing them outside of the toolbox.

"What must be in here?" I asked, picking up some of the loose screws and placing them back in the old pill bottles our dad used to house his assortment of nails and screws.

Van Gogh squatted, studying the license plate.

"A flathead should do it," Van Gogh announced, bouncing back up and pulling out different sized flathead screwdrivers. He laid the screwdrivers on the ground and got to work, sliding a screwdriver into one of the license plate screws and rhythmically turning it counterclockwise.

"Why are you taking off the license plate?" I asked while he plucked out the first screw.

"To make it harder to track down Dad's car," he said, working on the second screw. "Hey, can you see what's in the glove compartment? I think Dad kept a set of maps in there."

When I eased the glove compartment open, a mess of papers flew out. Dad was anything but tidy, so the series of maps forced to fold against the original symmetrical creases and pink crumpled, expired insurance cards falling onto the passenger seat was expected.

"Find anything?" Van Gogh called from the back.

"Yeah," I called back, scooping up the maps.

Van Gogh held Dad's license plate in his hands as he eased the trunk closed with his elbow.

It took us a while to refold the warped maps into their rightful creases so that they would fit into our backpacks. Once we were done, Van Gogh opened the car door and surveyed both the front and back seats.

"I think that's everything," he said, grabbing the rest of the papers on the passenger seat and closing the car door.

"What are we doing, Van Gogh?" I asked, more exhaustion in my tone than I intended there to be.

As he began ripping up the expired insurance cards, he looked out at the horizon.

"We need to throw these away, and then get rid of this license plate," he said, nodding toward the ocean. That's when I understood his plan.

"Wait, we're *leaving* the car?" I asked in disbelief. "How are we going to get to New York? I mean, we don't have a phone or a ride. Are we seriously going to *walk* to New York?"

Van Gogh sighed as he began walking toward the ocean.

I quickly followed after him, plunging the ripped, expired papers into a nearby trash can as I went.

"Wolfgang, they know that we're gone. It's only a matter of time before we are reported missing. You don't think they're going to discover that Dad's car is missing and try to track us down? We need to be untraceable!" Van Gogh exclaimed, marching forward, gripping the license plate.

"I know but—" I began, but stopped, struggling to find the right words. "It's just that... I just don't know how we're going to survive." I lowered my head as we continued to move toward the ocean.

Van Gogh didn't respond. Instead, we moved at a steady pace until we were within a few feet of the body of water. Then he took a deep breath while looking down at the license plate.

"Wolfgang, do you trust me?" he asked.

"Always," I said without skipping a beat. Even though my response was quick, I wondered if it was thought through. Of course, I trusted my brother, in that I trusted he would always try to protect us. However, did I trust that his plan was the *right* plan? I really couldn't say, but I knew that I *had* to trust him because if not Van Gogh, then who? We only had each other.

Van Gogh nodded as he took a step back and flung the license plate into the ocean as if it were a frisbee.

The license plate soared over the lapping waves and landed somewhere on top of the ocean's watery surface. I imagined the plop of the plate landing on top of the ocean's body, but this sound was drowned out by the rhythmic ebb and flow of the tide.

"Trust that we will make it to New York. We will find our mom. We have to. There is no turning back," Van Gogh said, as he placed his hand on top of my shoulder.

I don't know how long we remained in the position, but once the sun set, Van Gogh turned around, and we began our journey to New York on foot.

SIX

BEGINNINGS TO ENDINGS

When the sun finally set, we needed to rely on the illumination of the streetlights—which were few and far between—to see where we were going. Trying to use our maps at this point was useless, as we didn't have a flashlight. We could've used the flashlights on our phones, but that idea was literally thrown out the window. Actually, we could have done a *lot* more on our phones, such as call a Lyft or an Uber. But now, we were forced to travel on foot. I didn't even know if telephone booths existed anymore, and if they did, neither of us knew the number for a Lyft, Uber, or even a taxi company.

So, we continued to keep moving forward, but this seemed pointless to me as we didn't know our exact location; I didn't even know if we'd made it out of Florida yet. It would take a miracle to find our way to the Northeast.

After walking a few miles, we came across a brightly lit neon sign that flashed "motel vacancy." Even in the dark, my look of exhaustion must have been luminous. The blanket of fatigue felt heavier with each step, and the additional weight of the paperback books in my backpack didn't help matters. As I instinctively slowed my pace and stared longingly at the vacancy sign, Van Gogh sighed and said we could rent a room.

I couldn't help but smile as we walked closer to the motel.

I was worried that we would need to show our IDs to rent a room. Surprisingly, as soon as Van Gogh took out his money and asked the price, we were led to a vacant room.

The pulsating neon-amber light felt like a beacon, guiding us to a place to rest. Van Gogh didn't need to say anything for me to know that we would only be here for one night, but at least we would not be wandering around in the dark.

Everything in the motel room seemed to match the neon-amber vacancy sign, except for the walls, which were a dusty beige, the wallpaper of which was clearly peeling away. Van Gogh placed his backpack on one twin bed, and I placed mine on the other. It took everything in my power to not collapse on that bed then and there.

It felt good to ease my shoes off as I pulled down the bedspread. Before Van Gogh could flip the light switch off, I nestled into the firm mattress and pulled the blankets up over my head.

It was the rhythmic coughing that I heard first, followed by the hooting of owls and the distant sounds of cars driving into the night. I didn't know whether I was awake or in a lucid dream, until I looked over at the bedside digital alarm clock. The blazing **2:00 a.m.** felt unmistakably real. I fought the urge to be pulled back into my slumber, but it was too strong.

2:15 a.m. The edges of consciousness began to form as I heard the noise once again. The beat was steady but not rapid. The coughs came far apart but were distinctly dry and close by.

I turned on my side to see a lump of blankets with a clump of dark-brown hair sticking out from underneath them.

"Van Gogh," I whispered a little too softly, as the lump did not budge. Clearing my throat, I said, "*Van Gogh.*"

The lump stirred and my brother's head popped out from underneath the blankets.

"Wolfgang?" he asked groggily. "What's wrong? You okay?"

"Funny, I was going to ask you the same question," I admitted, sitting up. "I thought I heard you coughing."

Van Gogh cleared his throat, turning to face me. I couldn't see his features, as the room was practically pitch-black. Although the curtains were pulled open from the only window in our room, the mixture of moonlight and neon-amber only illuminated the small TV, its stand, and the chairs facing the bed.

"Maybe. I was asleep. You should be too. We have a long trip ahead of us." Van Gogh began turning over and pulling the blankets up over his head.

"Okay," I said, resigning myself to sleep, but what once was so easy to do now eluded me. Unfortunately, all I could do was shut my eyes and long for rest. I even tried squeezing my eyes shut and telling myself to sleep but it was no use. Unceasing thoughts, which mostly came in the form of doubts and questions, came to the surface and wouldn't submerge.

I couldn't help but wonder what would happen to us, and how we were going to find our mom. These questions were an infinite merry-go-round, unwavering in their insistence to come round and round, ceasing to stop. In response to my questions, I told myself, *Van Gogh will get us out of this. He will figure this out.* It was like I was repeating this assurance to myself over and over, but to no avail. *How? We have never done this before. How can I be so certain, so* sure *that Van Gogh will get us out of this?* I asked myself, waiting for an answer. *He's your brother, that's why. He will figure it out.*

That was my inevitable answer, said only to silence my worries and to embody our mom's only guidance, "breathe deep and swim." However, to swim with Van Gogh was to swim in uncharted waters. To swim was to risk everything, but what "everything" was at this point in time was *us*. We were everything to each other, and that was why I kept coming back to it. *He's your brother.* Van Gogh was more than my brother though, he was my only family. Even if we found our mom, Van Gogh was still the only family I knew—besides Dad and Uncle Earl, who were both long gone.

Although I never said it, I wished we could just try to make it on our own—but if we were to choose that route, we'd need to live off the grid because there was no way that any state would allow a sixteen-year-old boy to raise his fourteen-year-old brother. Sure, we'd probably inherit our grandparents' house, but Van Gogh didn't have a job, so he couldn't support us. However, knowing my brother, he'd probably drop out of school to get a job. I could never expect him to make that sacrifice. Van Gogh had made too many sacrifices in his life, and I knew that he would make more, but upending his future just so that we could stay together was a sacrifice far too large.

Van Gogh aspired to go to art school. Although he didn't talk about it as much as he used to, I knew this was still his dream. I also knew Janelle was the one who inspired him to have this dream.

One night, before Van Gogh's arrest, he'd met Janelle while he was tagging a wall. Apparently, she was walking home when she stopped to admire his work.

That night, when he snuck in through our bedroom window after curfew, he practically spent the whole night recounting their time together.

"She asked if *Starry Night* was my favorite painting, or if I just had a thing for post-impressionism," he raved, his eyes as starry as his namesake's famed painting. "I told her I was tagging my real name, to which she said, 'So, you *are* a post-impressionist graffiti artist then.'"

"Keep it down. Dad will hear you," I'd said, placing my bookmark in *The Outsiders*. It was one of the first seventh-grade summer assigned readings that I'd chosen to read over and over again to the point that I could practically recite the opening lines.

"I don't care," Van Gogh asserted, hiding his spray cans under his bed. "I would do it again, especially tonight."

"You just met her," I pointed out. "I don't get it."

Van Gogh smirked as he sat beside me and ruffled my hair.

"You will one day," he stated, almost as if his opinion was a fact. "One day, you'll find someone that you'll really care about, someone that attracts you to them in a way that is magnetizing."

"So, she's cute," I inferred, smoothing down my hair.

Van Gogh looked out our window, gazing at an indiscriminate point, as if he were looking out far beyond the present view.

"She is most definitely beautiful, but it's more than that. There's something about her that just pulls you to her. She's amazing without me knowing why, but I'm determined to find out." He'd gotten up from my bed then, adding, "I will most definitely find out." It was as if he was making a promise, perhaps to himself, perhaps to Janelle, perhaps to both of them. But whoever the promise was to, he'd kept that promise.

Every night, Van Gogh had snuck out of our window at the same time to find Janelle, and every night he'd returned, frowning, reporting that he didn't find her. It was not until his first day of high school that he found her in art class.

Although Janelle was not Van Gogh's first crush, he felt the need to describe her in vivid detail. He first noticed her golden eyes, which matched the strands of gold in her curly brown hair. He told me how her eyes smiled when she was sketching, and that even on the first day of school, she was already drawing in her sketchbook before the class had even begun.

Although Van Gogh was in high school and I was still in middle school, we'd continued to ride on the same bus as the middle and high school were only about a couple of blocks apart. Since we lived in a small town, we only had one middle and one high school, both of which looked like stubby redbrick buildings.

It was on our bus that I first met Janelle. My brother and Janelle were still friends at the time, but I knew he was trying to woo her. Well, I said he was wooing her, but he said he was trying to get her to go on one date.

"It's on the first date that you spark," Van Gogh had explained, "and then, that's it. You're just together. It's that simple."

Only Van Gogh could reduce being in love to something that easy. Almost everything seemed to come easily to him, though, so it didn't surprise me that he thought being in a relationship would be that easy for him.

When we got on the bus, my brother and I sat right in the first row, me to the right side in the first two empty seats, and Van Gogh right next to Janelle, who was already sitting on the left side, right behind the bus driver.

"Wolfgang, this is Janelle Achebe. Janelle, this is my younger brother, Wolfgang Amadeus Mozart Thomas."

"Wow, that is some name," Janelle had said as she tucked a strand of hair behind her ear. "What do you want me to call you?"

I opened my mouth, but quickly closed it, not expecting this question. Usually, people called me "Wolf." Only Van Gogh called me "Wolfgang," and he normally introduced me by rambling off my full name. He never told me why he did that, but I suspected it was to confirm my namesake.

"It doesn't matter," I said as I looked down at my backpack. "People usually call me Wolf."

Janelle paused for a second. Out of the corner of my eye, I could feel her studying my face, but not in a probing way. It seemed gentler, as if she were trying to understand my response by looking at my profile.

"Okay, but what do *you* prefer to be called? I really don't care what everyone else does. It's your name, so you should decide how people say it," Janelle suggested as she continued to look at me, waiting for an answer.

I turned to see Van Gogh smiling at Janelle. It was at that moment that I knew why he liked her so much. Similar to him, she did what she wanted to do, despite others' judgment, despite rupturing social norms. Like my brother, she was her own person, and defiantly so.

"Wolfgang," I stated decisively. "I prefer to be called by my full first name."

"Ah, so the others are your middle names, like the composer," Janelle surmised. "You were named after Mozart, right?"

"Right. You're probably not named after him, but are you related to Chinua Achebe?"

She blinked a few times before responding.

"No, it's a pretty common Igbo name, though," Janelle acknowledged. "You've read Achebe?"

"Only *Things Fall Apart*."

"Wow, that's a pretty advanced book for a kid your age—I'm impressed," Janelle stated, smiling. "And I'm not easily impressed."

Janelle's smile was soft and comforting, and her eyes glinted in the sunlight pouring in from the windows—but it didn't look like her eyes were *smiling* to me. Nevertheless, I was not infatuated with Janelle, like Van Gogh. However, I could tell that she really liked him from the sheer fact that she spent most of the bus ride trying to get to know me.

"Hey, I haven't seen you on the bus before," I noted.

"I usually don't take the bus," Janelle admitted, turning toward Van Gogh. "But the bus has become more appealing than my mom's car."

As I observed both of them looking into each other's eyes and blushing, I knew that Van Gogh had succeeded in wooing Janelle. It was not long before they went on their first date, and then their second, third—and fiftieth, even.

Even though older brothers typically leave their younger brothers, and close friends, behind once they begin dating a girl, Van Gogh was not a typical older brother, and Janelle was not a typical girlfriend. They both invited me to go to the park, movies, or wherever they were headed. Their invitations never felt forced. Even though they both loved to spend time alone, they genuinely seemed to like it when I tagged along. Although I loved hanging out with Janelle and my brother, sometimes I turned down an invitation, stating that I had homework to complete, so they could have some time alone. I think they both knew what I was doing, as they would smile and say they would see me later.

Their friendship with me, and their relationship with each other, seemed effortless. Van Gogh and Janelle were enamored with one another for over a year, and their love seemed seamless. They didn't emanate the raw passion of teens in lust, but rather acted like a couple that had grown into and with each other—as though they'd known each other their entire lives. Perhaps it was for that reason their breakup was so surprising.

The beginning of the end started with a simple question.

"When are you going to introduce me to your dad?" Janelle had asked as she took a sip of coffee. She'd cupped her coffee mug as she looked straight into Van Gogh's eyes. He didn't look away, but from the way he gripped the handle of his mug, I could tell he wanted to. I looked down at my cereal, feeling the weight of the loaded question.

By this time, Van Gogh and Janelle had been dating for over a year. He was regularly invited to Janelle's house. I had even gone over to her house a few times. From the minute I entered the Achebes' foyer, I knew that I was entering a different world. Our pale-green, one-story house could literally fit inside her Victorian home.

My first impression of her house was that it was as grand as a castle, but the pastel-colored furniture and perfectly set thermostat made the large house feel less grandiose and much cozier. Her mom only enhanced the sense of comfort when she greeted us. When I'd first met Janelle's mom, Fabiana Achebe, she literally welcomed me with open arms. Janelle had definitely inherited her mom's smile, as well as her mom's sense of compassion and openness. But her candor was definitely inherited from her dad, Kambili Achebe.

"Come in, boys, come in," Janelle's mom had said, as she gestured toward one of the elongated couches in the living room.

I saw Van Gogh wiping his palms on his khakis as he walked over to the couch. This was probably the first and only time—outside of a funeral home—that I saw my brother in anything other than jeans.

"Can I get you anything?" Janelle's mom asked, looking from Van Gogh to me and back again.

"No, thank you, Mrs. Achebe," I said.

Janelle's mom smiled as she ran her fingers through a strip of long, wavy blonde hair hanging over her shoulder.

"Oh, please call me Fabiana, everyone does," she stated. "Are you sure I can't get you anything? I can make up a fruit plate in a snap." Before we could respond, Mr. Achebe placed his hand on Janelle's mom's knee and said that he'd help with the fruit plate in a minute.

"So, what are your intentions with my daughter?" Mr. Achebe asked, leaning forward, waiting for Van Gogh to respond.

Mr. Achebe's eyes perfectly matched his daughter's. His gaze was steady. I could see him sizing up Van Gogh before my brother had a chance to respond.

Before I'd met Mr. Achebe, I knew he'd immigrated with his family from Nigeria when he was younger than Janelle. In fact, Janelle told us how her parents met in law school, similar to how Van Gogh and Janelle met when he was tagging a wall, except her dad was on his way to his dorm when he found her mom painting part of a banner for an upcoming dance. Also, similar to Janelle, her mom asked about Mr. Achebe's first name. It was almost as if history was repeating itself with Janelle and Van Gogh's "meet-cute."

"I really like Janelle. No, I really *love* her," Van Gogh asserted, matching Mr. Achebe's gaze.

To that, Mr. Achebe smirked and nodded.

"That's what I said when I first met Fabiana's dad," Mr. Achebe offered. "It takes a lot of courage to speak your mind like that. I'm impressed—and I'm not easily impressed."

Van Gogh's gaze seemed to lessen in intensity as he relaxed his shoulders and took Janelle's hand in his. After the first time I came to Janelle's house, I didn't see Mr. Achebe that often, but when I did, I sensed a certain camaraderie between Van Gogh and Mr. Achebe. Perhaps this was why Janelle was so open about her family's past, more open that Van Gogh was about ours by far. Initially, I didn't think that this bothered Janelle, until that day in the café.

"Van Gogh, did you hear me? When are you going to introduce me to your dad?" Janelle had repeated. She furrowed her brows as she waited for his response.

"I don't know," he finally said. "I'm not sure it is a good idea."

Janelle's eyes narrowed as she leaned back.

"Why?" Her tone was daring and sharp.

"It's just not a good idea," he repeated, looking away. His gaze fell over my bowl of cereal. He stared at the submerging cornflakes. Part of me wondered if he wanted to join them as he searched for what to say next.

"I mean, you wouldn't want to meet him. He's not the easiest person to get along with."

To that, Janelle relaxed her brows and reached for Van Gogh's hand, which she gently held in hers.

"Look, I know you don't get along with your dad, but if he's your family, I don't care. I love you, and he's a part of you, so we should meet."

Reluctantly, Van Gogh nodded, agreeing that they could meet. This was his first mistake. The second was inviting Janelle to a family dinner.

Even though I'd never witnessed a train wreck, the outcome of that night was its metaphorical equivalent. Janelle had arrived at our house wearing a silky, blue dress and matching shoes. Her golden-brown, curly hair seemed especially springy as the ends settled on her shoulders.

When Van Gogh opened the front door, he was taken aback by her appearance—as was I, feeling that in her presence, we were severely undressed. At least my brother had the sense to wear his khakis, which were closer to formal than my jeans and T-shirt.

"Where's your dad?" Janelle asked, adjusting her thin purse strap on her shoulder.

"Oh, he's still at work, but he's coming," Van Gogh stated, taking her hand in his and walking her to the couch.

It was only that morning that Van Gogh had told Dad that he'd invited someone to dinner, and that someone was his girlfriend. From that, Dad learned that we were actually going to entertain—something that rarely happened in the Thomas household, unless you counted him inviting his friends over to watch the Super Bowl—and that Van Gogh had a girlfriend.

To our surprise, Dad didn't ask any questions when he heard the news. Instead, he just nodded and said he wouldn't be home too late.

Not being home too late turned into eight o'clock—one hour after Janelle had arrived. Van Gogh and I were smart enough not to call for takeout until our dad came home. When we were little, we'd eaten far too many pieces of lukewarm slices of pizza waiting for Dad to eat with us. We knew him too well to not continue to make that mistake.

When we heard the front door close, and our dad calling for "Van" and "Wolf," I looked over at Van Gogh, who seemed to squeeze Janelle's hand a little tighter as the both of them stood up.

Upon seeing Janelle, our dad stood silent. He seemed to look from Janelle to Van Gogh, but his gaze firmly rested on my brother, who stared back at our dad's matching lily-pad-green eyes.

"Dad, this is my *girlfriend*, Janelle," Van Gogh asserted, cutting through the silence. His assertion was quick but firm. Van Gogh made a point of emphasizing that Janelle was his girlfriend as he released her hand in exchange for holding her around her waist.

The only response that Dad offered was to continue to look Van Gogh in the eyes. Janelle quizzically looked from my brother to Dad as she took a step forward and extended her hand for a handshake.

"It's really good to meet you, Mr. Thomas," Janelle stated, offering her hand for a proper introduction.

For what seemed like an extended beat, Dad continued to look into Van Gogh's eyes, until the spell finally broke and his gaze dropped to Janelle's hand, which he shook without saying a word.

Janelle smiled, stepping back toward Van Gogh, who continued to look at our dad. I'd never seen his stare so focused, as though he were trying to communicate with our dad telepathically. He never shied away from telling Dad exactly what was on his mind, so I knew his silence was a form of restraint. This restraint was palpable, especially when we finally headed to the kitchen to sit at our makeshift "dinner table."

Our dinner table couldn't even compare to Janelle's family's elongated, glossy mahogany one. Instead, ours was a beige kitchen table with one leg off-kilter, which caused our food to slide unless we used a pack of Post-its to steady it.

We all sat at the empty kitchen table, the silence once again penetrating the air.

"Maybe we can order Chinese?" I asked, seeking any way to break the tension. I didn't even wait for an answer before I pulled out my cell phone and began to dial.

After I placed our order, Dad finally spoke.

"So, you two," he began, pointing his index finger from Van Gogh to Janelle, who were sitting adjacent to one another, "are dating?"

"Yeah, Dad, we are. That's what I told you this morning," Van Gogh asserted, taking Janelle's hand in his.

At that, Janelle looked over at Van Gogh in disbelief.

"Wait, your dad didn't *know*? We've been dating for over a year," Janelle stated, pulling her hand away from Van Gogh.

My brother's gaze softened as he looked into Janelle's widening eyes.

"Van Gogh, how can you not tell your *own father* about us?" Janelle asked, to which he noticeably swallowed. "Are you ashamed of us?" Janelle probed, crossing her arms over her chest.

My brother quickly said, "No, of course not. It's just—"

"What, Van Gogh, *what?*" Janelle pressed.

"It's that he knows it's not right," Dad interjected. "He knows this is wrong and it's not happening in my house."

The air felt constricted. I watched the wave of understanding wash over Janelle. Van Gogh slapped both palms against the tabletop, bolting upright. He almost toppled over his chair, glaring down at our dad, who was still sitting but staring straight into Van Gogh's searing eyes.

"Shut up," Van Gogh hissed. "What's wrong is *you*. That's why I didn't introduce you to Janelle."

"No son of mine is going to date a Black girl," Dad declared, his words hammering into the tense atmosphere.

Before Van Gogh could respond, Janelle said something about having to leave and ran out of the house. With a furious, and disappointed, look at Dad, my brother flew out of the house, chasing after Janelle.

It was over three hours later when Van Gogh returned. Alone.

The untouched Chinese takeout containers remained in their paper bags on the kitchen table. Retrieving the food was the only time I got up from my seat. Soon after Van Gogh left, Dad said he was going out, and mumbled something about me never bringing home a Black girl, to which I said nothing.

My lack of a response continued to haunt me.

Although I didn't love Janelle like Van Gogh did, I loved her unwavering acceptance and compassion. I had never met someone who reserved judgment until she really knew a person, or who never made assumptions that would inevitably lead to harmful, hasty generalizations. She never judged me for tagging along with her and Van Gogh. She never asked me why I read so much or asked why I didn't act like a "normal kid," unlike my dad who seemed to *only* ask me that question.

Aside from Van Gogh, she was the only other person who accepted me for exactly who I was, which was why when Van Gogh plopped down at the kitchen table and told me their relationship was over, I felt like I was in a swirling cocktail of shock, sorrow, and loss.

"What do you mean 'it's over'?" I asked in disbelief. "What happened?"

Van Gogh began to take the Chinese takeout containers out of the bags and place them in the fridge.

"It's just over." He'd sighed, balling up the paper bags and throwing them into the trash. "She said that she couldn't be with me if that's how my dad felt about us."

Van Gogh stared down at the kitchen tabletop, but his gaze didn't seem fixed. His searching eyes glanced over the whole table, not really settling on a specific point.

"But you don't agree with Dad. *I* don't agree with Dad. Why should his opinion matter?" I asked, to which Van Gogh's heavy, exhausted eyes looked into my insistent gaze.

"It doesn't to me, but it does to her," he explained as he got up. "She said that she does not want to put either of us in a situation where we are fighting that type of discrimination from my own father. I said I would leave, that I would somehow emancipate myself, but it didn't matter—she said you could never truly leave family behind. Look, it's late. I'm going to bed."

As Van Gogh walked to our bedroom, I couldn't help but feel a sense of sorrow mixed with relief. Sorrow for my brother, for losing the only girl that he'd ever loved, who was probably his soulmate. Sorrow for me, for losing an older sister because even if we weren't related, she treated me with the same kindness my brother always had, and always will.

And relief for myself, because even though Van Gogh chose Janelle over our family, she wouldn't let him do so. Because she broke his heart, I wouldn't be left behind.

SEVEN

LOCKED SECRETS

6:00 a.m.

The red digital numbers were more pronounced than the emerging dawn sunlight. Normally, 6:00 a.m. would be an unknown time that existed in a world somewhere outside of my state of consciousness. Normally, I'd be curled up under my covers, unaware that the persistent, blazing alarm would sound off in an hour. But after finding our dad dead in his bedroom and abandoning everything we knew in search of Mom, what was once normal for me wasn't anymore.

I spent most of the night in and out of consciousness in microsleeps, only to fully awaken at 4:00 a.m. Realizing that sleep was elusive, I picked up *Madame Bovary* and managed to finish the novel. As I closed the book, I couldn't help but reread one of the last lines my mom had highlighted and underlined: "A final spasm threw her back upon the mattress. They all drew near. She ceased to exist." Although this line didn't mark the ending of the book, it did mark the ending of Emma Bovary herself. However, unlike the other lines Mom marked—to which she included her inferences and reactions—this line was emphasized with no explanation as to why it was important to her. Perhaps she marked this line to note where and when Emma Bovary died, but I couldn't help but wonder if there was more to it than that. Could Mom have related to this line on a personal level? Did she connect this line to another text or situation? Similar to my mom, this would remain a mystery.

Even if we did find Mom, I was certain she would still be this unknown person who happened to be my blood relative. At this point, without really knowing who she was as a person, she was a means to an end. She was a means to staying with my real family—Van Gogh.

6:05 a.m. The series of coughs coming from under my brother's covers kept surprising me as the sound broke through the silence at unpredicted intervals. I did not know whether or not Van Gogh was awake, but the covers only seemed to move when he was coughing.

Once the covers stilled, I placed *Madame Bovary* back into my backpack. I got up and tried to tiptoe toward the bathroom as quietly as possible, but nevertheless, at the squeaking of the mattress springs, my brother began to stir.

"Wolfgang?" Van Gogh asked, pulling the covers down. "What time is it?" As he asked, he looked over at the alarm clock, discovering the answer for himself. He wiped the sleep from his eyes as he shook his head and sat up.

Van Gogh coughed into his arm as he stood up and pulled on his socks and sneakers. He was still wearing the same blue T-shirt and jeans that he'd been wearing when we left our house.

As soon as he stood up, he fell back onto the bed, shaking his head. I ran to him, standing at his side.

"Are you okay?" I asked, hesitating to hold out my hand, knowing that Van Gogh would brush it away. Van Gogh did not consider himself to be "tough," but he was also reluctant to accept help unless he absolutely needed it.

"Yeah," he affirmed, rubbing his eyes, which seemed teary and red. "I just stood up too fast."

I nodded, not really believing him but not really knowing what else to say or do. Almost as if he were reading my mind, he asked me if I wanted any breakfast.

Once again, I nodded.

"Just give me a minute and we'll get something. We'll take a shower and change first. Who knows when we'll be able to do that again," Van Gogh stated, unzipping his backpack and pulling out a change of clothes, another blue T-shirt—except this one had a picture of *The Beatles* on it when they played on the *Ed Sullivan Show*—along with another pair of jeans, socks, and boxers. He also pulled out two toothbrushes, one of which was mine, and toothpaste.

"Maybe we could stay another night?" I asked, taking my toothbrush as he handed it to me. "I mean, Mom's not going anywhere."

Van Gogh shook his head as he placed his clothes next to him.

"It won't be too long," he said. "We'll make it to New York before you know it." I knew that Van Gogh was trying to exude confidence in his tone, but a thick ribbon of doubt was sewn into his words.

Looking down at his open backpack, I shook my head. That was when I saw the locked wooden box that I'd found in the back of Dad's closet peeping out. As if compelled by some unknown force, my hand reached inside and pulled out the box. It was much larger than the palm of my hand, but it felt light and it was shaped like a glossy oak cube. It was practically symmetrical, except for the dangling brass combination padlock on one side. I turned the box around in my hands until I was staring at the lock.

Once again, a flood of questions invaded my thoughts.

Why was this box in the back of Dad's closet? Who did it belong to? Did it belong to Dad? To Mom? Why was it locked? What was inside?

Perhaps Van Gogh had a natural knack for reading my mind, or maybe I was just that easy to read. Nevertheless, as he was also studying the box, he stated, "It probably belonged to Mom."

I turned it over in my hands once again, searching for any other distinguishing marks that may indicate who the box belonged to, an inscription or a label.

"How do you figure?" I asked, finding nothing other than the lock.

"Well, it was near our birth certificates and that picture of Mom holding you. I mean, since it was next to Mom's stuff, it only stands to reason that this was hers," he reasoned, nodding toward the bathroom. "Go on, get ready. The sun's coming up."

We definitely had enough money for a hearty breakfast, but Van Gogh was insistent about being as frugal as possible. "We need to spend this on essentials," he explained. I wanted to explain that food was essential, but I let it go.

At the nearby diner, we ordered two cups of black coffee and two bowls of cereal.

I could hear and feel my stomach growling before our breakfast arrived. As the waitress poured our coffee, I was relieved to hear that refills were free.

"Don't drink too much," Van Gogh warned as he sipped his coffee. "Too many bathroom breaks will slow us down." After setting the mug down, he rubbed his eyes and then unzipped his backpack to pull out one of the maps.

"Are you okay?" I asked as he began to unfold the map.

"Yeah, I'm just tired, that's all," he admitted, studying the unfolded map that acted as a makeshift tablecloth. "Did you sleep okay?"

I shook my head, feeling the curtain of muggy exhaustion hanging over me. My brother's exhaustion seemed to reflect mine, but his seemed more intense, as if I were looking into a concave mirror, magnifying his fatigue. His green irises seemed to be surrounded by thin, squiggling red veins. They'd seemed much redder in our room, however, but that may have been because of the red interior. His eyes were no longer watery, but the dark circles underneath were an even darker shade of purplish gray. His face seemed gaunt and pale, but that could have been from a lack of food. He hadn't coughed since we left the motel, but that could be because he was stifling his coughs. Every once in a while, I saw him forcibly swallowing even when he was not drinking anything.

When the waitress placed our twin bowls of cereal in front of us, we both said thank you. I moved my dry cornflakes around with my spoon to give them a coating of milk as Van Gogh pushed his bowl aside.

"Aren't you hungry?" I asked with the first spoonful of cereal in my mouth.

Van Gogh nodded as he placed his fingertip on an area of the map.

"Van Gogh," I said a little louder, to which he looked up. "Aren't you hungry?" I repeated, nodding toward the bowl.

"I'm just figuring something out," he said distractedly, furrowing his brow and continuing to draw an imaginary line on the map with his index finger.

"Are we still in Florida?" I asked, my mouth filled with another spoonful of cornflakes.

"I think we are close to the state line, if we haven't passed it yet."

"Wouldn't we have known if we passed it? I mean, wouldn't there be a sign?" I asked, shoveling in another spoonful.

From the vivid descriptions I'd read about in books, I felt as though I'd traveled to different countries, decades, centuries, and even different worlds—but this was merely in my imagination. Neither Van Gogh nor I had ever been outside of Florida until now.

"Normally, yes, but we walked a lot, so it's possible we passed the state line and just didn't realize it."

I looked down at my half-empty bowl of cereal, absentmindedly shoveling spoonful after spoonful into my mouth. If I were more of an optimist, I would have considered it to be half-full. Either way, I knew it was not enough. I glanced over at Van Gogh's untouched bowl of cereal, guiltily longing for a second bowl or some pancakes.

He must've been looking over at me because the next thing I knew, he was pushing the bowl toward me.

"Here, I'm not that hungry anyway," he claimed, taking another sip of his coffee.

"If we're going to continue to walk, you're going to need your strength," I stated, reluctantly pushing the bowl back toward him. "Is that the plan?"

"No. Do me a favor—lift your bowl and mug," he asked, folding the map back up and stuffing it into his backpack. He once again pushed his bowl of cereal to me. "I think there's another way."

"What way is that?" I sighed, pulling his bowl closer and plunging my spoon in.

"Well, if we can find a train that will take us to New York, then I think that's our best bet. We can pay in cash, and we won't need any ID to buy a ticket."

I let his explanation sink in as I felt a sense of relief at the thought of sitting in a train car instead of walking thousands of miles northeast on foot.

"Now, we just need to find the right station," he said, taking another sip of coffee.

"How are we going to do that?" I asked between spoonfuls of cereal.

"I'll figure it out," Van Gogh stated, grinning. "Don't I always have a plan?"

I nodded, stopping myself from asking any additional questions. *Trust him, trust him. He knows what he's doing,* I told myself, trying to suppress any sense of doubt or concern.

"Do you know who I was thinking about?" I asked, changing the subject to get my mind off our journey. "Janelle."

At her name, Van Gogh's gaze drifted toward the window, where he watched the vivid, fiery auburn sun lick the blue blanket of sky.

"What made you think about Janelle?" he asked. His tone must've been softer than he intended because he quickly cleared his throat.

I shrugged, placing my spoon in the now empty cereal bowl. I longingly looked into both bowls, wishing they had been bigger. At least I felt fuller than I did before.

"I don't know," I lied, refusing to acknowledge what had triggered the memory. "It was just one of those things, you know? Your mind just sort of wanders, especially when you can't go to sleep. She just popped into my head."

He nodded, still looking at the horizon.

"Do you ever think about her?" I asked.

Van Gogh hadn't mentioned Janelle ever since they broke up. I wasn't sure whether or not he'd ever come across Janelle in the cafeteria—as

juniors and seniors shared the same lunch period—in the hallways, or
if they were still in art class together. However, I did know that she no
longer took the bus to school.

Now that Van Gogh and I were both high school students, I figured
I would see Janelle in the hallways, but school had just begun only a few
weeks ago. However, now that Van Gogh and I were headed to New York,
it was doubtful that we would ever run into Janelle. Although we'd left
on a Saturday, the school was bound to look for us as the absences began
piling up.

"Sometimes," he confessed, his gaze drifting away from the view and
hovering over his coffee mug.

"I miss her," I added, and then winced, wishing that I could take that
back. "I mean, I don't *really* miss her, I just remember when we hung out,
and I miss *that*."

Van Gogh gave me a half smile as he lifted the coffee mug to his lips.

"It's okay," he said, taking a sip. "She really cared about you. She once
said you were like the brother she always wanted."

To this, I smiled, seeing a flash of the three of us in the park, wishing
that I could rewind time, to go back to a moment where my worries
seemed few and far between.

Van Gogh unzipped his backpack and pulled out the locked
wooden box.

"So, I think we need to get this open," Van Gogh asserted, holding
the box out. Now it was his turn to change the subject.

His brows furrowed as he turned the box around so the lock faced
him. He lifted the lock as if trying to pull it but its shackle was securely
fastened, fulfilling its purpose to keep whatever was hidden inside a secret.

"You don't happen to know how to crack a combination lock, do you?"
I joked, half wondering if he did.

Van Gogh smirked, placing the box on the table. "No, but we'll get
it open."

"What do you think is inside?" I studied the thin line where the lid
of the box separated from its body.

He picked up the box, shaking it. "Don't know."

Whatever was inside the box didn't make a sound.

"It's possible it's empty," he said, placing the box back in his backpack and zipping it up.

"No," I said, somehow certain. "I'm sure there's something inside."

I couldn't discern why I was so certain that there were contents within the box, but nevertheless, I understood this to be a fact. If Van Gogh were right, and this was our mom's box, then why would she lock it if it was empty?

Maybe my certainty came out of longing for discovery. If the box's contents gave us insight into our mom, then maybe I would feel a greater sense of connection to her. Perhaps the items would even give us insight into why she ran away, why she chose to abandon her family for another life.

EIGHT

ARE YOU OKAY?

"So, you boys are headed up to New York then?" the motel front desk manager asked, typing on his keyboard from behind the plexiglass shield.

Van Gogh reluctantly affirmed that this was true. Usually, he would never ask anyone for directions. Similar to our dad, he stubbornly relied on his keen sense of direction, so to them both, *actually* asking someone for explicit directions was akin to admitting defeat.

However, we both knew that we would need more than good luck and an internal compass to find our way to New York, so we had no choice.

"Hmm, I think the Silver Meteor is your best bet. Do you know where that is?" the manager asked, looking away from his screen. The manager's thick, blue-rimmed glasses magnified his dark-brown eyes, which looked from Van Gogh to me and back again.

"No," Van Gogh reluctantly acknowledged. "But I'm sure that we can find it."

"It's at the Winter Haven Station. That's not too far from here—maybe about a mile away," the manager said as he took off his glasses, the lenses of which were beginning to fog up from the breath emanating from his matching light-blue mask.

"Damn masks are driving me nuts!" he exclaimed. "I can barely see because these things keep fogging up." He extended his glasses out to us from inside the plexiglass shield.

"I had a friend who had the same problem," I said, remembering Sophie, who was severely myopic and constantly complained about the same issue. She also had to ensure that she could breathe in the mask, as she had asthma and initially made the mistake of wearing a mask that had constricted her breathing, causing her to cough and wheeze.

Before Sophie had been adopted, she wore plastic black frames that could barely fit around her thick lenses. However, once she was adopted, her new parents paid for a new pair of glasses, with trendy black frames and flattened lenses.

"If you lift up the mask a little more, and make it a little tighter, your glasses will hold the mask in place so the air doesn't really escape from the top. You can also wash your lenses in warm water and dish soap. This acts like an antifog solution."

Van Gogh turned to look at me, and tilted his head, as if nonverbally questioning how I knew how to do this, since I had never worn glasses. Reading his expression, I admitted that Sophie told me, to which he nodded.

"Thanks...?"

"Wolfgang," I offered, to which I felt Van Gogh's elbow nudge me in the ribs.

"That's a nickname," my brother said. "He wants to be a musician."

The clerk let out a "huh" as he tightened and pulled up his mask.

"That's pretty different. Usually kids your age want to start a rock band or something. I haven't heard of too many wanting to become classical pianists. That's pretty classy, kid—I mean, *Wolfgang*."

"Yeah, he's one of a kind," Van Gogh quickly stated, grabbing my elbow and backing away from the motel reception desk. "Well, thank you for the information...?" The manager pointed to his nametag which read "Jonathan."

"No problem," Jonathan said. "You know, my shift's almost over. If you boys are not in a hurry, I can drive you to the station. It's on my way."

"Oh no," Van Gogh stated, taking another step back from the desk. "That's too much trouble—"

"No trouble at all!" Jonathan responded, walking around from behind the desk. "I insist. The day manager is on in a few. Why don't you boys sit in the office and wait for a bit? It won't be too long."

Before Van Gogh could say anything, I quickly exclaimed, "Thank you, Jonathan, that would be great," to which I received another nudge in my ribs, except this one was applied with a bit more force.

"What are you doing?" Van Gogh whispered, as we followed Jonathan to the door behind the front desk.

Without answering Van Gogh, I followed Jonathan into the office. It was no bigger than a walk-in closet, but it felt even more cramped with the small, gray desk facing one wall, the tiny flat-screen TV propped up above the desk, and the plaid love seat facing the TV screen. As I sat on the couch, I placed my backpack on the floor between my legs. Van Gogh reluctantly sat next to me as Jonathan repeated that we would leave very soon. Then, he went back to the front desk, leaving us alone.

"Hey," Van Gogh asserted, pulling down his N95 mask. "Are you going to tell me exactly what you are doing?"

I looked into his bloodshot green eyes, which seemed unusually sullen under his heavy eyelids. At that moment, I was certain of two things: One, I knew that if we walked to the station, Van Gogh probably wouldn't make it. Ironically, even though he seemed to be sleeping when I was awake, he'd barely got any sleep, either. And two, I knew that I couldn't tell Van Gogh the real reason why I accepted a stranger's offer to take us to the train station because he would never admit that he was too tired to continue walking.

When our dad first started showing signs of COVID-19, Van Gogh had been frustrated because Dad refused to accept medical attention and wouldn't even admit that he was sick. Part of me thought that Van Gogh was so angry at Dad about his unwillingness to take care of himself because he saw a reflection of himself in Dad's stubbornness. Similar to Dad, Van Gogh hated to admit when he was ill, or when he was feeling weak. Although my brother wasn't a "tough guy," he did see himself as the strong one. He relied on this strength to make his way in the world, and I guess so did I, because without his stubbornness, ingenuity, and fortitude, I didn't know where I would be.

I knew I had to choose my words carefully, because if I didn't, Van Gogh would march us out of the office to walk on foot to the station.

"This will help us get there faster," I explained, watching the open door to ensure that Jonathan couldn't hear us. "Who knows how long it would take us to get to the station if we walked there? This is easier," I said, picking up the remote on the love seat's armrest and quickly turning on the TV before Van Gogh had a chance to answer.

"You are too trusting, Wolfgang. You don't even know who this guy *is*, I mean—" But before he could finish his sentence, a picture of two boys appeared on the screen. Both were lanky and staring straight into the camera but neither of the boys was smiling. The one with the lily-pad-green eyes and short dark-brown hair was taller than the boy with the light-blue eyes who stood next to him. They were standing in front of a pale-green, one-story house. *Our* pale-green, one-story house. The picture didn't capture this, but I knew this picture was taken right before our Uncle Earl died, as I couldn't remember Dad taking any pictures of us at any other time.

Both Van Gogh and I leaned forward as we listened to the news report.

"The missing sons of Benjamin Thomas—who was discovered in his home by his employer, Grayson Tanner, after passing away from the coronavirus—were last seen in the video footage we gathered from a gas station off of US-27 North," the news anchor stated. "What you are about to see is truly remarkable." The next thing we knew, the scene switched to a distant clip of Van Gogh aiming our dad's shotgun at the gas station thief. As the clip played on, we heard the news anchor's voiceover: "After speaking with the clerk, it seems that the older of the two boys prevented the criminal, identified as Joseph Kent, from robbing this station. Thanks to this boy's brave efforts, the criminal, who had robbed ten gas stations prior to this one, was finally arrested."

The clip ended the same way it began, with Van Gogh's unwavering hold on the shotgun, pointed directly at the thief.

"If you know the whereabouts of these boys, the older of whom has been identified as Van Gogh Vincent Thomas, and the younger as Wolfgang Amadeus Mozart Thomas, please contact this station," the news anchor concluded, as the news station's website and number flashed on the screen.

I felt my jaw hang open, which was the polar opposite of Van Gogh's tightly closed mouth. His green eyes were glued to the screen as I quickly pressed the power button, which caused the screen to fade to black and become eerily silent.

My heart raced to a speed that felt faster than a cheetah's run as I squeezed the TV remote.

Van Gogh finally blinked and roughly ran his hand through his hair as he said what summed up our joint feeling at that moment. "Shit."

To be frozen without actually undergoing the process of freezing is the best way to describe how I felt at that moment. I wanted to move, to do something, *anything* but my body was stuck in that position, firmly holding the TV remote in my hand, still aimed at the blank TV screen. My rapidly beating heart never felt more pronounced. This feeling severely contrasted the stillness in that room. The sounds of routine, of organic and inorganic movement, was severely absent, leaving only two runaways staring into nothingness, lost in a thought that wasn't really a thought, but rather a state of mind that signified the realization that they had been discovered.

"Shit," Van Gogh repeated, roughly running his fingers through his hair. I couldn't help but feel a sense of relief that the silence had been broken. However, this did not quiet the anxiety I felt, or the image of my brother standing with our dad's shotgun poised at the thief. "This is bad."

"I know," I acknowledged, lowering my head to look down at my backpack, which was nestled between my feet on the floor.

"I mean, we don't know how long that has been playing," Van Gogh said, leaning back on the love seat. "We don't know how many people have seen this."

"Well, I think it's a local news station. At least it's not CNN," I offered, knowing that this fact didn't change anything.

Whether this story was reported locally, nationally, or even internationally, we *knew* people were looking for us. Although the photograph displayed had been taken a few years ago, we didn't look that different. Perhaps we were a few inches taller, but otherwise there was no question that the boys in that picture were us. Although the news station chose to only show that one clip of Van Gogh holding the thief at gunpoint, who knows how much video footage the news, the police, and social services had. We were surrounded, which was only a prelude to being physically surrounded, and we both knew it.

"Okay," Van Gogh said at last, standing up suddenly. "We have to get out of here."

I finally released my grip on the remote by placing it on the armrest, and I picked up my backpack.

"How?" I asked, standing up. "Do you think he heard anything?" I nodded toward the ajar office door.

"I don't know, but either way, we can't risk going with this guy." He placed his N95 mask on his face, easing his backpack onto his shoulders. "We have no other choice than to walk."

The purplish-gray circles under Van Gogh's eyes seemed even darker, more distinct, especially in contrast to his white mask. An overwhelming feeling of helplessness crept up my spine. I surveyed the office, as though one of the few objects or pieces of furniture would inspire a plan of my own. But the desk covered with files, the plaid love seat, and the black TV screen offered nothing.

All I could do was reluctantly nod. Once again, I was confronted with the bitter taste of lacking a choice, of having to shove my instincts down and follow the leader.

"You have everything, right?" Van Gogh asked, to which I nodded. "Good, just follow my lead."

I followed him as he casually walked out of the office.

Jonathan was still at the desk, checking someone in.

"Hey, so we called a taxi because we saw that you're busy," my brother said, as he continued to walk backward toward the motel exit. Before Jonathan could respond, Van Gogh took my hand and waved as he said, "Thank you for the offer, though! We really appreciate it!" I could imagine the look of my brother's false smile painted on his face underneath his mask as we quickened our pace.

As soon as we were far enough away from the motel, Van Gogh pulled out one of the maps from his backpack. We continued to walk as he unfolded the map in front of him.

"It looks like the station is on 7th St, South West," Van Gogh said, tilting the map slightly to the left and squinting. "Like Jonathan said, it's only a mile. If we continue to take this road, we should see it soon. If we see a store, let's stop in."

"You want to go to a store? Why?" I asked.

Van Gogh rubbed his eyes as he placed his hand on my shoulder, pocketing the map. I could feel the pressure of his weight pushing me down, which I think was unintentional. I had the sneaking suspicion he didn't place his hand on my shoulder to reassure me, but rather to help himself maintain balance.

"We can get some supplies—like water and food, whatever we can find. Plus, we need to figure out how to disguise ourselves. Maybe there's something we can find in a store that can mask us somehow," Van Gogh pondered. As though reading my mind, he added, "Aside from our *actual* masks. Those may not be enough."

I cringed, thinking of a passage from S.E. Hinton's novel, *The Outsiders*.

"You're not going to make me cut or bleach my hair, are you?" I asked.

I could hear Van Gogh laughing from underneath his N95 mask. "Only if you *really* want to. What would make you think that I would make you do that?"

"Well, that's what Johnny made Ponyboy do in *The Outsiders* to disguise themselves."

My brother laughed again before saying, "You really think art imitates life, don't you?"

"Yeah, sometimes. I mean, it almost worked for them," I said, knowing that it hadn't. It was an impulsive and ineffective plan. Despite changing their appearance, they were eventually discovered because of their heroics.

"Van Gogh, do you regret what you did at the gas station?" I asked, reflecting on my brother's own heroism.

"No, it had to be done. Otherwise..." He shook his head, as though rethinking his response. "It just had to be done, that's all."

Even though Van Gogh didn't finish his sentence, we both knew what he was going to say. Knowing nothing about the thief, his actions were unpredictable. He probably had never fired his gun before because he had unwittingly left the safety on. However, maybe he would have discovered this error, and maybe he would have rectified it in the moment that he held me at gunpoint.

Now, we had to face the consequences of escaping death—trying to escape capture and inevitable separation.

As we continued to walk, I surveyed the area, seeing rows of auburn, gold, and green leaved trees lining our gray pavement path. I had to slow down my pace so that I didn't pass Van Gogh, who was lagging. Although I was fast—which may have been why our high school track coach asked me to try out for the team—my brother had always kept up with me. Also, I couldn't help but notice that he was no longer trying to suppress his cough.

Before we reached the train station, we managed to find a pharmacy where we bought a pair of cheap sunglasses, two matching blue baseball caps, two bottles of water, and more trail mix. I was tempted to put a bottle of cough syrup on the counter as well, but I didn't want to raise the suspicions of the cashier or Van Gogh. He had managed to prevent himself from coughing in the store, but once we were outside, he let out a series of rapid, dry coughs into his elbow.

I placed my hand on his back as we both waited for the coughing to stop.

"Let's sit down," I suggested, nodding at the curb.

I was surprised that Van Gogh let me lead him as we both sat on the curbside, watching cars drive by.

After what felt like five or even ten minutes, Van Gogh finally spoke.

"I'm okay, you know," he claimed, pulling off his N95 mask to take a swig of water.

"Are you *sure*?" I asked, a little more pointedly than I meant to, but I didn't relent. "You don't sound fine. You sound … well, you sound sick."

Van Gogh turned to face me. His green-lily-pad eyes—a little dimmer—thoughtfully stared into mine.

"It's a cold, that's all," he explained, placing his hand on my shoulder. From his light touch, I could tell that this time, he wasn't trying to regain his balance. On the contrary, he was trying to provide me with a sense of reassurance. "I know we're living in a scary time, for more reasons than one. I also know that a lot has happened to both of us in only a couple of days. But that's life. The one constant in life is change, and we're caught in a monsoon of change right now. But you know what?" Van Gogh wrapped his arm around my shoulders. "We'll survive it. Do you know why?" I shook my head. "We'll survive it because we have each other, and that's all we really need. If we stay together, we can weather any storm. Got it?"

I lowered my N95 mask to smile at my brother, whose own smile mirrored mine.

As we sat on the curb, with Van Gogh's arm still wrapped around my shoulders, his coughing subsided. Part of me wished that we could just stay here, not moving toward a destination or trying to evade anyone. Remaining invisible observers who watched the world change from a distance but were not part of the change—the *devastation*—would be the closest notion of an idyllic existence. However, I knew the ideal was in no way realistic. The *real* world was fraught with change. It was a milieu of positive and negative forces that eventually create a sense of balance from the disruption.

As we stood up to continue on our journey, I longed to find a change that brought about hope instead of anxiety. In the meantime, I just needed to breathe deep and swim to find the finish line.

NINE

A TICKET TO RIDE

The Winter Haven Station reflected the same color pattern of its Amtrak train, except for the orange roof of the station house, which was in a darker hue.

I lifted my sunglasses to observe the light and dark contrasts. With the afternoon Florida sun blazing, I doubted anyone would question our choice in eyewear. Both Van Gogh and I stared up at the Amtrak sign, as though to confirm its existence. *We were here. We made it.*

Despite Van Gogh's sporadic coughing and obvious fatigue, he'd made it. I should never have doubted him because his mix of fortitude and stubbornness could get him through anything. We did end up stopping periodically to take rests, at my request, so it wasn't until late afternoon that we finally reached the station.

When we walked into the station house, it didn't take us long to find the ticket booth. We were greeted by a young ticket salesman, who, based on his uniform, could be mistaken for a conductor.

"How can I help you boys?" he asked, typing on his keyboard from behind the plexiglass barrier.

"We'd like two tickets to New York—one adult and one child," Van Gogh said. Glancing at me, he added, "He's fourteen, so that would be a child's ticket, right?"

The man nodded as he typed. "Do you want to go to the New York State Fair Station or Penn Station?"

"Which one takes us to New York City?" My brother asked as the ticket salesman typed something else into his computer.

"You want Penn Station," he confirmed. "That'll be a direct connection. It'll take approximately twenty-four hours to arrive at Penn Station. When would you like to leave?"

"As soon as possible," Van Gogh insisted, pulling the money out of his backpack. The brim of his cap cast a shadow over the thinning wad. "Do you take cash?"

The ticket salesman narrowed his eyes and furrowed his brow in suspicion. I felt my heart sputter in my chest. *Did we really make it all this way only to get caught now? Was this where our journey ended? Had this man seen us on TV somehow?*

The salesman's fingers hovered over his keyboard, and I prepared for defeat—only for him to shrug, as though talking himself out of his suspicions. He continued to type.

"Yes. There's a train that leaves in a couple of hours, but there's limited seating. You're traveling together, I assume?"

"Correct," I affirmed. "We're brothers, so we'd like to sit together if possible, please."

"Yes, that's no problem. Coach or a room?"

Van Gogh glanced down at the thinning wad of cash in his hands before asking, "Which is the cheaper option?"

"Coach. There are only a few remaining coach seats next to each other. Okay, two coach seats. Are you choosing to protect your trip?"

"What does that mean?" Van Gogh asked, thumbing through the bills in his hand.

"Protecting provides you with insurance for loss, damage, or theft of your belongings. You will also receive a reimbursement for eligible meals and accommodations if the trip is delayed. And it provides you emergency assistance, all day and all night. We highly recommend this protection, but it will come at an additional $90 charge per traveler."

I could see Van Gogh shaking his head slightly, but before he could respond, I whispered, "*Please*, Van Gogh, we have enough. The motel wasn't that much. Let's just see how much it is."

Van Gogh sighed, looking from the bills to the ticket salesman. "Okay, we'll take the protection."

"Very good," the ticket salesman replied, continuing to type. "Now, while on the train, you must wear your face mask at all times and sustain social distancing practices. Have you experienced any COVID-19 symptoms within the last fourteen days or knowingly had contact with anyone diagnosed with COVID-19 in the last fourteen days?"

Without even skipping a beat, Van Gogh let out a firm "no" as I watched him swallow. *Technically* Dad hadn't been diagnosed with COVID-19, but we both knew that he had it, and according to the news, he was diagnosed posthumously. But we were smart enough to know that we couldn't admit this, otherwise we'd *never* make it to New York. And so, with insurmountable guilt, I repeated "no," swallowing hard as I committed to the lie.

"In the case where you do not comply with our health and safety protocols, we have the right to remove you from the train. Do you understand?"

We both nodded.

"Okay, you're all set. That will be $500," the ticket salesman revealed. He waited to print out the tickets until Van Gogh paid. Van Gogh swallowed once again as he folded the approximately $200 we still had and shoved the bills into his wallet.

"Thank you for traveling with Amtrak," the ticket salesman stated robotically, pushing the tickets out from the small opening at the bottom of the plexiglass barrier.

Van Gogh folded the tickets and shoved them into his pocket, and we walked to the platform.

◦◦◦

We both placed our backpacks between our legs as we sat on the black and blue benches. The unyielding wood felt good as I leaned back.

I looked over at Van Gogh. With the blue baseball cap and wide sunglasses nestled over his N95 mask, I barely recognized my own brother. However, for me, the distinct blue *The Beatles* T-shirt was an apparent giveaway, as I knew that my brother was a huge fan.

"Do you think that he recognized us?" Van Gogh asked, lowering his mask to take a sip of water from his half-empty bottle.

"I don't think so," I answered. "I mean, between the sunglasses and the caps, *I* hardly know that we are who we are. I think we're safe."

Van Gogh nodded, coughing again. A few passersby slowed their pace, glaring fearfully his way before pushing into a speed walk, clutching their masks to their mouths.

We finally had tickets to New York, and I should've felt relieved about that—but I couldn't help but wonder how our actions may be putting others at risk.

Leaning closer to my brother, I lowered my voice so no one could overhear me. "Van Gogh, do you feel guilty about lying?"

He looked around. There were a few people nearby, but they were standing well out of earshot.

"We didn't really have a choice, did we? I mean, if we would've told that ticket salesman about Dad, he never would've let us on the train. Plus, we were careful around Dad. There's no way that we could have caught it," he said with certainty.

Yes, we were both safe—but we'd inevitably put ourselves at risk by staying in the same house with Dad, and that couldn't be argued against. However, what choice did we have? We hadn't had anywhere else to go, and even if we'd found another place to stay, Dad would never have allowed it. Plus, although we were both living with him, it was Van Gogh who was more at risk of contracting COVID-19 from the sheer fact that he was the one taking care of Dad.

Even before Dad contracted COVID-19, I hardly went into his room. However, after we knew Dad was ill, Van Gogh practically made it a quarantined area—especially near the end, when Dad no longer had the strength to leave his room. Prior to that point, it was practically impossible to keep Dad in the house, as Van Gogh had tried to do several times. For as long as he was physically able, Dad went on with life as though nothing had changed. He went to work, to the grocery store, to the gas station, exposing himself to so many innocent people.

What if we were now doing the same thing?

"I can't believe you're still going to work," Van Gogh scoffed, placing his sketch pad on the table at the sound of the closing door.

We heard Dad's dry coughing fit before we saw him walk into the living room and sit on the armchair, adjacent to the couch.

He took a few deep breaths before answering.

"It's nothing—I just have a cold." But his words were interrupted by bouts of coughing, and I couldn't remember a cold I'd ever had that did that. "Maybe I'm getting asthma, but that's all."

Van Gogh gave Dad a once over, looking from his tan boots caked in dirt, to his worn-out jeans, plaid shirt, and matching jacket. Dad's green eyes were bloodshot and dim from a combination of illness and inebriation. Either way, he obviously didn't look fit to work.

"I don't know if Grayson is ever on site, but if he is, he must be blind," Van Gogh said with a scoff, standing up and marching toward our room.

Without missing a beat, I followed my brother as our dad sunk into the armchair and searched for the TV remote.

"Do you know what time it is?" Van Gogh asked, pulling me out of the memory.

I shook my head, hoping the train would arrive soon.

We must have sat on that bench for at least two hours before the train pulled into the station. The entire time we waited, I listened to Van Gogh's muffled, dry cough. As I listened, I couldn't help but wonder whether or not my brother's cough was just that—or something more.

TEN

UNLOCKING SECRETS

Our seats were close to the bathroom, which was not an ideal spot—but at least when we needed to use the restroom, it was convenient. The gray seats were firm but comfortable. Although, I could foresee that comfort waning thin and feeling the need to stretch my legs if this is where we would have to sit for the next twenty-four hours.

Our backpacks were small enough that we were able to bring them with us on the train, but they were too large to keep under our seats, so we stuffed them in the overhead baggage area. However, before placing them overhead, I pulled out one of the books I had yet to read: Arthur Miller's play, *All My Sons*. Van Gogh took out Mom's wooden box as well as one of Dad's maps.

We both pulled our trays down and placed our items in front of us. Opening Miller's play, I wondered what the tiny white plane and upside-down building signified as well as whether or not Mom had annotated this book, too.

Aside from the color of my eyes, this was something I'd obviously inherited from her—the need to annotate. I know that most people didn't do so, but I annotated every book that piqued my interest, whether or not it was a school-assigned text.

The description of the setting at the beginning of Act One was vividly detailed. I immediately recognized the neat, curvy script next to a portion of a descriptive sentence that she'd underlined: "…the terrible concentration of the uneducated man of whom there is still wonder in many commonly known things…" Next to this line, she'd simply written, "*Dad.*" Was it possible she was referring to *our* dad? Sometimes married couples called each other "Mom" and "Dad," as if by being married parents, they magically became their own parents. But this didn't seem likely, considering in an annotation in *Madame Bovary*, she had written our dad's name next to a line. It was possible that she was referring to *her* dad. Similar to our mom, her family was a mystery to both Van Gogh and me. Of course, we knew that she had a family, but we had no idea who was a part of this family.

Van Gogh and I had only known our dad's family, which basically consisted of Uncle Earl. We never knew their parents because they died before our time. However, it was very possible that, unbeknownst to us, we had an extended family on our mom's side. Did we have *living* grandparents? Another uncle? An aunt? Possibly even cousins? There was also the possibility that our mom remarried. *Maybe* we even had half-siblings.

"Van Gogh, do you think we have any brothers or sisters we don't know about?" I asked as I felt the train begin to slowly move forward.

"Maybe," he said, refolding the map. "I mean, anything's possible. Why do you ask?"

"Well, I started reading one of Mom's books—*All My Sons,* by Arthur Miller, who may or may not be related to Mom—and she wrote "Dad" next to a line. It just led me to question whether or not we have an extended family that we don't know about. I mean, it *is* possible that Mom ran away *because* she fell in love with someone else."

As Van Gogh paused to consider this, my eyes were drawn to the mysterious wooden box with the brass lock.

"I mean, it's possible that if we could get that open," I went on, pointing at the locked box on Van Gogh's tray, "we could find out more about her."

My brother slid his fingers between the lock and the box. "I agree, but neither of us knows the combination, and I don't know how many numerical combinations we would need to try to open it." His thumb caressed the numbers, feeling its ridges.

"Well, if this really is Mom's box, then maybe she's the one who set the combination. If that's the case, maybe it's a combination we know."

Van Gogh nodded, clearing his throat, swallowing hard. I could tell that he was trying to suppress his cough again.

After about a minute, he placed the box on my tray, put his up, and stood up to fish his nearly empty water bottle out of his backpack. He gulped down the rest of the water. When I told him he could have mine as well, he shook his head.

"I'm going to throw this out," he said as he eased his N95 mask back on and stood up to find a recycling bin.

As he walked down the aisles, I stared at the lock. The numbers were evenly separated from one another and were carefully etched into the thick metal loops.

I began to randomly spin the circular metal with my thumb.

1-1-1-1. No. **1-1-1-2.** No. **1-1-1-3.** No.

Are you going to try every *four-digit combination?*

What else can I do?

A question with a question, without any answers.

So, I continued in that way, trying every random four-digit combination. I had finally reached **1-1-2-2** when Van Gogh returned.

"Any luck?" he asked as he sat down.

Shaking my head, I narrowed my eyes from behind my sunglasses as I stared at the stubborn lock.

"This may take the whole train ride," I said, knowing in my heart that we'd be lucky if we cracked this code at all, let alone during this train ride. "I mean, that is unless she *did* set it herself and it *is* a four-digit combination that we know."

Van Gogh crossed his arms over his chest.

"Well, if that's the case, then let's try years. Try 2006," Van Gogh instructed.

"The year I was born?" I asked as I rotated the metal loops. "Nope. 2004?" I eased the last loop slightly back. With the number four prominently displayed, I pulled on the lock again, but to no avail. "You don't think it could be the year she left, do you?"

"Doubtful but try it."

2-0-0-9. No.

"Try our birth years backward," Van Gogh instructed.

4-0-0-2. No.

6-0-0-2. No.

"Well, maybe she used her own birth year, or even birthdate. Try 1978. I think that's when Mom was born."

Pulling off my sunglasses, I looked over at him quizzically, to which he shrugged. "What? I wasn't as young when she left. I remember a few things from when she still lived with us. They got married when she was twenty years old and Dad was twenty-two." As I continued to look at him with my questioning gaze, he stated, "I asked, okay? Look, stop looking at me like that, and try it."

1-9-7-8. No.

"Let's try the year they got married then," Van Gogh instructed once again.

1-9-9-8. No.

"Dad's birth year?" I asked as I began spinning the numbers into place.

1-9-7-6. No.

Van Gogh leaned back, swallowing hard once again, and shaking his head.

"Take my water bottle," I insisted. "I don't want anymore. It's in my backpack. Please, take it. We can probably get more if we're thirsty."

Van Gogh reluctantly stood up. As he stood in the aisle and fished inside my backpack, the train was quiet enough for me to hear Van Gogh unzip, zip, unzip, and rezip my backpack a few times.

"Did you find it?" I asked.

Van Gogh moved back into his seat, holding my nearly full water bottle and two slips of folded paper.

After Van Gogh took a huge gulp of water, he twisted the water bottle cap back on, and placed the two slips of folded paper on my tray.

As I unfolded the first sheet, Van Gogh stated, "Maybe there's something in here that will give us a clue."

Once I unfolded the paper, I recognized it immediately.

"You think a clue is in your birth certificate?" I asked.

"Or yours," Van Gogh added, leaning over to unfold the other sheet of paper.

Studying Van Gogh's birth certificate, I found a series of numbers: his birth date, time of birth, the document number, birth number—whatever that was—the date and time that the birth certificate was filed, our parents' ages at the time of his birth, the hospital's address and our parents' address. Most of the number combinations were either too long or too short for the four-digit combination that was needed to unlock Mom's lock. I began by rotating the metal loops to form Van Gogh's birth month and day.

0-8-2-1. No.

Backward.

1-2-8-0. No.

"Try the time of birth then," Van Gogh stated.

1-0-3-1. No.

Backward.

1-3-0-1. No.

"Try yours," Van Gogh insisted, pointing at my birthdate.

I shrugged.

"Okay, but I think it's a long shot," I asserted.

Usually when people use personalized combinations, they use memorable numbers—numbers that are precious to them—to create these combinations. These are secure, trustworthy numbers that will keep their secrets safe. I couldn't help but wonder why our mom, who abandoned her two children, would use any number connected to either one of us for her combination lock.

"Humor me, okay? Try your birth date first."

0-2-0-2. No. Unsurprising.

Backward.

2-0-2-0. No.

"Okay, try the time of birth."

Searching the birth certificate, I found the time of birth right next to my birth date.

0-3-1-9. *Yes.*

ELEVEN

AN EPISTOLARY JOURNEY

The opened lock, still hanging from its latch, was nestled in my hand. Still in disbelief, I didn't try to remove it and ease open the wooden box. I just sat there, once again frozen.

"I don't understand," I mumbled to nobody in particular.

"I guess she did use a special combination," Van Gogh responded.

I shook my head, letting go of the lock, allowing it to dangle from the latch.

"No," I asserted. "It's just a coincidence."

Van Gogh reached over and eased the lock out of the latch and placed it on the tray.

"Maybe, but that would be *some* coincidence, don't you think?"

I nodded, flipping the latch up and opening the lid of the box with both of my thumbs.

The color of the inside of the wooden box replicated the outside, except the inside didn't have a glossy finish, but the wood was equally smooth. Peering at the box's contents, it was no wonder that we hadn't heard a jingle or a clang when the box was shaken, because none of the objects were metallic. In fact, the box mostly contained cards stacked one on top of the other, a couple of small, square photos, and two strips of plastic with a bunch of holes horizontally punched into one side of the strips.

Van Gogh picked up the two strips of plastic, studying the middle of each, which contained a barcode.

"Do you know what these must be?" Van Gogh asked, and then quickly answered his own question. "These must be our hospital bracelets. Look." He pointed above the barcodes at our names, which were typed with our surnames followed by our first names. Our date of birth and the word "male" was printed just between our names and the barcode.

"Why do you think she kept them?" I asked.

"I mean, we are her sons," Van Gogh said, shrugging. "This is a great find. When we find her, we can show her these," he added, holding up the strips, "and it will help convince her to take us in."

I shrugged as Van Gogh carefully folded our hospital bracelets and placed them back into the box.

Next, he picked out the photos, giving one of them to me to study while he studied the other. Van Gogh pulled off his sunglasses and placed them on the tray in order to get a better look. I cross-referenced the photos we each held, and it was obvious that they captured the same event.

In my photo, two people were in front of a church, both of whom stood on the beige stone steps leading up to the church's entrance. The woman was veiled and wearing a long, silky white dress that hid her shoes, which presumably matched her formal wear. The man standing next to her held her waist lovingly. He wore a charcoal three-piece suit and a matching bow tie. It was difficult to tell, but I imagined that from under the veil, the woman was looking directly into the camera lens, as was the man standing next to her. Although I couldn't tell whether or not the woman was smiling, the man seemed genuinely happy as he faced the camera with a wide grin on his face.

Even though I barely recognized the veiled woman, the man's lily-pad-green eyes were a dead giveaway.

"This must be Mom and Dad's wedding picture," I told Van Gogh.

"And this"—he gestured to the other picture, where our parents stood among a few other people dressed in gowns and three-piece suits—"must've been their wedding party."

In the picture Van Gogh held, our mom, now unveiled, stared directly into the camera lens, her blue eyes practically glowing as she smiled.

Although I immediately recognized our Uncle Earl—who apparently *would* be caught in a suit alive—who stood to the other side of our dad, I didn't recognize any other member of the wedding party.

While Dad stood to Mom's right, three other people stood to her left, all of whom shared her soft, light-blue eyes. One was a man, who had Mom's high cheekbones and thin build, except he was a lot taller than she was. In fact, he was probably the tallest person in the picture. The other two people near her were women. The older woman had thick strands of gray streaking her shoulder-length, light-brown hair, and the other woman, who was shorter and heavier, looked to be about Mom's age, maybe even a little younger. Both were wearing matching floral gowns as they held matching bouquets and smiled at the camera.

"Do you recognize the other people in the photo?" I asked Van Gogh. He shook his head and turned over the picture to study the back, where we found our mom's neat, curvy script. *Wedding Day, February 2nd, 1998.*

"Hey, you were born on their anniversary!" Van Gogh exclaimed. "Who do you think wrote that?"

Without missing a beat, I said, "Mom. That's definitely her penmanship. It matches her annotations."

Van Gogh nodded, taking a look at the picture I held. Flipping it over, we found the same inscription.

"Well, whoever those people are, they look exactly like Mom, so you were right. We *definitely* have an extended family that we've never met. At least, I don't remember meeting any of them."

"Me neither," I admitted.

After taking one last look at the photos, Van Gogh placed them back in the box, exchanging them for the stack of cards, which took up most of the space inside the box.

Van Gogh quickly opened and closed each card, written in black ink, and each beginning with the greeting, "Dear Ann."

"These must be to Mom," I said. I knew I was stating the obvious, but I needed the verbal confirmation.

I pulled out the card from the bottom of the stack, figuring that this card was written first. We both looked at the cover, painted with clinking champagne glasses, with the inscription "Happy Anniversary!" written underneath. In the right-hand corner of the left side of the card, the sender wrote the date:

February 2nd, 1999
Dear Ann,

Your first anniversary is one of the most memorable milestones. I remember when your father and I celebrated our first anniversary. It was truly a magical event. We took the train down to the city, but he wouldn't even tell me what we were doing until we reached our destination. He just told me to bring a heavy coat, gloves, and a warm hat. Similar to your wedding, ours was also in the dead of winter, so what else would I wear? From train to train, he could not stop grinning until we finally reached our destination, Rockefeller Center. When we arrived, he said, "Rose, may I have this dance?" Looking out onto the ice rink, I had no idea what he was talking about—that is, until we rented a pair of skates and glided all over that rink, as if we were dancing. It was truly the most memorable night of my life, not counting the birth of you, Alan, and Marilynn. You are all my life, but so was your father. He was such a romantic during the first years of our marriage. I know that you both did not always see eye to eye, but he would have loved to see you get married, God rest his soul.

Relationships are tricky, whether they be parent-child relationships or romantic ones, but as long as we love the other person, then we will make it through anything. Your father may not have had the exact words to say this, but he was so proud of you, Ann. Please know that.

I wish you a lifetime of love and happiness with Benjamin.

Love Always,
Mom

As Van Gogh's eyes shifted from left to right, I could tell that he was still reading when I finished the first card. I was grateful that I had a moment to process the content of the card on my own.

I'd assumed that I had a maternal grandma, but I'd had no idea that her name was Rose, or that her husband—our mom's father—died before our parents were married. Also, who were Alan and Marilynn? Were they the two people in the photograph?

Before I could ask Van Gogh any of these questions, we heard the call of the conductor as he yelled, "Tickets, please! Have your tickets out!"

I wasn't sure whether or not Van Gogh had finished reading the card, but he immediately looked away from it and fished our tickets out of his pocket. It wasn't soon after that the conductor walked up to our row and asked us for our tickets.

Van Gogh looked up at the conductor, whose mask matched his dark-blue uniform, and handed him the tickets. The conductor pulled out a handheld machine and scanned the tickets before placing them into his coat pocket.

I said, "Thank you," expecting the conductor to quickly move on to the next passenger, but he seemed to linger. His small brown eyes squinted, flitting from Van Gogh to me and then back to Van Gogh.

"Do you boys usually take this train?" the conductor asked, to which Van Gogh and I both shook our heads.

"No, this is the first time we are taking this train," Van Gogh said, looking away from the conductor and surreptitiously placing his left hand over Mom's card.

The conductor hummed. "You both look familiar."

"Well, we probably just have those kinds of faces, you know?" my brother suggested.

The conductor stood in the aisle for what felt like another minute, but it was probably just a few seconds, before he said, "Have a great trip," and moved down the aisle, requesting to see more tickets.

As soon as the conductor was out of earshot, Van Gogh whispered, "Put on your sunglasses." He slid his on.

"Do you think he recognized us?" I asked, placing my sunglasses back on and pulling down my cap a bit, feeling the cloth hugging my skull.

"Maybe," Van Gogh speculated. "We need to be careful. We have no idea who saw that news report, or how many times it will play."

"Well, once we get out of Florida, I think we'll be safe. I mean, how likely do you think it is that anyone outside of the state saw that clip?" I asked, wishing I could see Van Gogh's expression as he looked at me from behind his dark sunglasses.

"Who knows," he said. Then he leaned in close and whispered, "I mean, consider the facts. We are minors whose father was featured in a COVID-19 news story, *and* we are responsible for the capture of a known thief who robbed several other gas stations."

"*You* are responsible for his capture," I corrected. "You are like a local hero."

Van Gogh leaned back and tilted his head up as he continued to speak to me. "Yeah, some hero. I can barely get us across the state line, and I'm the hero."

"Hey, we *are* going across the state line," I reminded him. "Plus, because of you, we were able to open Mom's box and get *that* much closer to figuring out who she is."

Van Gogh looked down at the card for a few more moments before looking up. I waited for his reaction as I adjusted my sunglasses, which were sliding down the bridge of my nose that wasn't covered by my mask. I quickly pulled the mask up, wishing that I could take it off. I dreaded keeping it on for twenty-four hours straight, until we reached New York.

"Have you ever heard of Grandma Rose?" I asked.

"I don't recognize any of these names," he admitted. "I mean, I don't remember Mom talking about her family. It's possible that she did, just not with me. It *is* possible that she mentioned them, but I just don't remember."

"What does it mean?" I asked, as if Van Gogh would have the answers that I sought.

"I don't know, but we *do* know that our maternal grandfather is no longer alive, and that Mom didn't get along with him."

"Like mother, like son," I quipped, to which I imagined Van Gogh rolling his eyes in response.

"*And*, that Mom isn't an only child, so that means we have an aunt and an uncle, who were probably the other two people in the wedding party."

The moment he said this, it all seemed so obvious.

Those people *had* to be Mom's siblings, Alan and Marilynn. Who else would look so much like her other than her siblings? Sure, sometimes cousins can look alike, but it was far more likely that these individuals had a closer relation to Mom.

"What does this mean?" I asked, not really knowing what else to say.

Van Gogh shrugged. "Don't know. Maybe another card will help answer that question."

I pulled another from the bottom of the stack. The green and red cover, stamped with a decorated, lit pine tree, was inscribed with the greeting, "Merry Christmas!" in bold, matching red and green script.

December 25th, 2004
Dear Ann,

I hope that you and Benjamin are enjoying your first Christmas with baby Vincent Van Gogh. I keep forgetting that the middle and first names were switched. I hope that you get around to fixing that soon. I still don't know why you insisted on naming your son after a crazed artist who cut off part of his left ear. Benjamin and I don't agree on much, but neither of us knows why you didn't pick a normal name for your son, like John or Philip. I know you've criticized me for naming you after a 1940s actress, but at least that's better than naming a baby after a suicidal artist. Well, as I always say, it's your life. I just hope that you have an answer for little Van Gogh when he asks about his namesake. I hope that you and Benjamin are patching things up. I know how distraught you were during our last phone call.

I know that you were hoping to come to New York this Christmas, but I also understand that money is tight. I wish I had money to send you, but your father didn't leave me with much. He was a good provider, but he didn't have much in the way of life insurance. It's around the holidays when I miss him the most.

Do not worry about me. I won't be alone on Christmas. Alan always comes by with Alice. Between you and me, I think your brother is going to propose to Alice this Christmas. When I ask, he tells me that he isn't ready to settle down, but I can see that spark in his eye when he looks at her.

We'll put a wreath on Daddy's and Marilynn's graves for you. I wish you the merriest of Christmases. Please send me pictures of little Van Gogh opening up his gifts and celebrating every moment of this special day.

Love Always,
Mom

And just like that, we lost an aunt that we never knew we'd had.

TWELVE

NAMESAKES AND KEEPSAKES

"I can't believe she died!" I exclaimed, closing the card. Shaking my head, I placed the cards we'd read back in the box. "I mean, I can't believe a lot, like that your name is not *technically* your name. It *is* your name, but not really."

For a few moments, Van Gogh didn't say anything. He just kept swallowing without drinking. He then twisted the cap off of the water bottle, pulled down his N95 mask, and took a long gulp of water.

With the water bottle nearly three-fourths empty—or one-quarter full, depending on your perspective—he twisted the cap back on and leaned back, pulling his N95 mask on, ensuring that the frames of his sunglasses were nestled over the top of the mask.

I resisted the urge to ask if he was okay because I already knew what he would say. I knew he'd insist he was "fine" and that he'd eventually get irritated by my asking the same question over and over—so I just looked back down at the other cards, waiting for his response.

"It's weird, but it makes sense," Van Gogh finally offered. "Vincent Van Gogh makes more sense."

"Why does that make more sense than its inversion?"

"Well, it's like your name, Wolfgang Amadeus Mozart. When you say your whole name, sure, most people know that you're named after Mozart, but with me, people immediately recognize my namesake's surname. 'Are you a post-impressionist artist?' they ask. No, not really. I mean, it's fine if they think I am, but I'm getting tired of that question."

I was kind of surprised by Van Gogh's response because he'd never said anything about his name. Even when Dad shortened it to "Van," he'd resigned himself to it.

"Isn't that kind of one of the first questions Janelle asked you when you first met?" I asked, regretting the question as soon as I asked it.

"Yes," he whispered, "but, that was different."

I waited for him to explain further, but he didn't offer anything more than that.

"So, you would've preferred to be named Vincent, then?"

Van Gogh shrugged, turning to face me.

"Maybe. I guess it doesn't matter because my name is my name, right? There's really no going back," Van Gogh said. "Now, your name, Wolfgang Amadeus Mozart—that's something."

I knew he couldn't see my expression, but I couldn't help but raise my brows from behind my sunglasses. "How so?"

"Well, you were named after this famed composer, but people wouldn't know that immediately. You can just go by your nickname, 'Wolf,' which sounds fierce—unlike mine, which just sounds like a mode of transportation. I mean, I'm sure you're not always questioned about your name, except when you give your full name, am I right?"

I nodded, never really thinking about my name from this perspective. I always questioned whether or not Mom believed I'd live up to my namesake. But since Van Gogh's name was accidentally inverted, maybe she *did* believe we could achieve the artistic greatness of our namesakes. Maybe by making their surnames our middle names, she was trying to keep this a secret, just between the three of us.

However, as fortune would have it, most individuals knew *exactly* who Van Gogh was named after. Even though Van Gogh didn't mention this, I wondered if he felt the pressure to live up to his namesake's reputation. Van Gogh wasn't the type of person to try to fit into any predetermined mold, or to try to live up to anyone's expectations—but every once in a while, maybe he did feel this pressure and simply never revealed it to anyone. Not even to me.

"Apparently, Mom wasn't too thrilled about her namesake," he went on. "I don't know which 1940s actress she was referring to, though."

"Hey, do you think Marilynn and Alan were named after an actress and an actor as well?" I asked, wishing I had my phone or a computer so I could look up the 1940s actress our grandma mentioned in the card. I didn't know if it would offer any insight into Mom, but it was something.

"Maybe Marilynn Monroe?" Van Gogh ventured, and then shrugged. "Alan is a pretty common name, so who knows?"

"Well…" I pulled another card out from the bottom of the stack. "We at least know that Marilynn died either before or around the time you were born, and that Alan is still alive … maybe."

Before opening the third card, we took a moment to look at the cover, which was covered in shiny blue balloons with the inscription "Congratulations on this Blessed Event!" underneath.

February 2nd, 2006
Dear Ann,

I am so glad that I am here for this blessed event! I know you're going to ask why I am writing my sentiments in a card when I'm here in person, but it has always been easier for me to write down my thoughts than to just go ahead and say them out loud. Wolfgang is such a beautiful baby. He looks exactly like you, Ann. Those light-blue eyes are yours. Those are Miller family eyes.

Holding that babe in my arms was like holding a precious treasure. He is surrounded by love. I have never seen Benjamin cry like that, but then again, you told me that he also cried when Van Gogh was born as well. I still question your choice in names, but again, it's your life.

Van Gogh was so enamored by his baby brother. You should see him, Ann. Van Gogh keeps trying to look into the nursery window to see Wolfgang. I have lifted him up a few times, as has Benjamin, so that he can take a closer look. I know it's too soon to tell, but I am telling you, those two will be inseparable, I can just feel it.

Your dad and sister would have loved to see your children. I imagine them looking down on them, sending them their blessings. Now, I know that you don't believe in that sort of thing, but I like to think that they are always smiling down on us.

Again, I am so glad that I was here for the birth of your son. After saying goodbye to Marilynn in an ICU, I just didn't know if I could ever step foot into a hospital, but I am very happy that I did.

I know that Alan is very sorry that he couldn't come. He just couldn't take the time off from teaching, but when I last spoke to him, he said that he sends his love.

Ann, this is another one of those moments that you will always remember.

Love Always,
Mom

While the card did not offer any additional insight into our mom or her siblings' namesakes, it did confirm what I already knew about Van Gogh: he would always watch over me. Apparently, he took this very seriously even at two years old.

It was surprising to learn that our dad actually cried when we were both born. I don't know if Van Gogh was as taken aback by learning this information as I was, but I never imagined that Dad would cry at our birth. I also could not fathom him lifting Van Gogh up so that my brother could look into the hospital's nursery. This action was so kind, so *fatherly.* It was completely out of character for our dad. However, it was possible that he'd had a profound change in character when Mom left—in a negative way. It was obvious that he'd grown bitter after she left him—left *us*—so maybe he'd been another person before her departure. Again, it was hard to imagine, but it was entirely possible.

"So, our uncle is a teacher," Van Gogh noted. "It seems like he's still alive here."

"Yeah, but what happened to Alice?" I asked. I scanned the letter once more but didn't see her name mentioned anywhere.

"Maybe it didn't work out," Van Gogh suggested. "Sometimes you think you're going to spend the rest of your life with someone, and then you just don't."

Like you and Janelle, I thought, but didn't say out loud.

"Well, maybe she just neglected to mention her," I ventured. "It doesn't *necessarily* mean that they didn't wind up together. I mean, the card wasn't really about Alan and Alice, it was about Mom and, well, my birth."

From his nod, it seemed that he agreed.

As I placed this card back in the box, I listened to the faint sounds in the background: the typing of keys on laptops, conversations that were too distant to discern any meaning from them, and the unzipping and zipping of carry-on bags. If I couldn't hear what others were saying, maybe they couldn't hear us either. We were just passengers in a crowded train, nothing more or less, which was exactly what we wanted—what we *needed*—to be.

"How many more cards do we have?"

"Three more," I answered. "I wonder why they are so spaced out."

"What do you mean?"

"Well, it's like there are gaps. I mean, we have a first anniversary card and two birth year cards. Did Grandma Rose only write to Mom because of these events, or are there other cards?" I asked, pulling the next card from the bottom of the pile.

"Maybe there were other cards, but maybe Mom only kept a few," Van Gogh ventured. "This looks like a keepsake box. People usually only keep important items in a keepsake box."

"Got it. How do you know about keepsake boxes?"

"Janelle used to have one," Van Gogh said, a little too nonchalantly. "She showed it to me a few times. That's where she would keep certain items. You know, ones that could fit in there, of course. I'm sure she didn't keep the ring in there though."

I shook my head, wondering if I'd heard him correctly.

"*Ring?* Do you mean—?"

"It was a promise ring," Van Gogh confessed, leaning back and tilting his head up. "I don't remember exactly when I gave it to her, but it wasn't too long before we broke up."

"A promise ring? As in a promise to be *engaged* some day?" I asked in disbelief.

"Yes," Van Gogh said, swallowing hard, followed by taking another gulp of water. "That's generally why you give someone a promise ring."

I knew Van Gogh loved Janelle, that he probably fell in love with her the first moment he saw her, but I never knew he'd intended to marry her someday. But really, I should've known. On the night that they broke up, he *did* intend to emancipate himself from our family to be with her, so I should've known he was fully committed to her.

"Would you have left me behind?" I asked, immediately regretting my question.

Van Gogh turned, facing me. I couldn't see his eyes from behind his sunglasses, but I could see his brows, which were furrowed with concern.

"What do you mean? That's why we're on this train, that's why we're headed to New York—so that we can stay together," Van Gogh explained, his brows still furrowed.

I shook my head.

"No, I know that," I said. "Not now, but back then. On the night that you and Janelle broke up. You said that you would emancipate yourself to be with Janelle. Would you have left me behind to be with her?"

Van Gogh's eyebrows seemed to relax as he placed his left hand on my shoulder.

"Wolfgang, I know it may have seemed that way that night, but I would have found a way to take you with us. That night might have been about trying to convince her to stay with me, but it was never about leaving you behind."

"But if you emancipated yourself, you wouldn't have emancipated me too," I reasoned.

"I know, but I would have found a way," Van Gogh asserted with such confidence, that I almost believed that he would have found some way to keep us together. "You trust that I would, right?"

"Yes," I said without hesitation. Even though I didn't know whether or not he would've figured out a way for me to live with him and Janelle, I recognized my brother's unwavering determination. I knew that he would stop at nothing to find a way to keep us together.

THIRTEEN

THE GRAY COFFIN

The cover of our grandma's next card was a somber white with the word "Sympathy" stamped in the middle.

March 29th, 2007
Dear Ann,

I know that nothing I write here can take away your pain, but our phone call felt unfinished. There was so much more I wanted to say, but I just couldn't find the words. I do wish that I could come to you right now. I so desperately want to get on a plane and hold you in my arms, but between my health and the expense of the airfare, that may not be possible at this time.

Even though I don't know what it's like to have a miscarriage, I do know what it's like to lose a child. It would take a series of lifetimes to recover from the pain. Neither loss is comparable, but they are both felt so deeply that the scars are in your bones, in your soul.

When Marilynn was sick, and we knew that she was going to die, there was nothing that anyone could say that could help me. I just needed to be alone. Even when I was with her in that hospital room, with Marilynn hooked up to a series of beeping machines, I felt so utterly alone. Yes, her body was there, but my Marilynn—the one who so enjoyed reading every book that she could get her hands on—was no more.

After she passed, I felt like I had an endless reserve of tears, but I could only cry when I was alone. When you or your brother visited me, I was putting on a show. I didn't even mean to do so, it just came naturally. We all grieve in our own way, and it takes some longer to recover than others. However, no one can deny that the pain of losing a child is so excruciating, that all of the words in any language are not enough to describe this horrific pain.

I know that Benjamin wants you to move on, and many will want you to come out of your mourning, but you do so at your own time. Ann, you have always been your own person. You have always done what felt right to you, no matter what anyone said, so do that now. Do what you need to do. Just breathe deep and swim, my darling little Ann.

Love Always,
Mom

Breathe deep and swim. I couldn't believe the only phrase I remember from Mom was given to her by my grandma. Was this a phrase that Mom adopted as her own? A phrase she took from her mother and passed on to us?

I looked for my brother's reaction, but with his sunglasses and mask covering everything but his brow, it was practically impossible to read him. If the phrase meant anything to him, I would just have to go ahead and ask.

"What do you think Grandma Rose meant by 'breathe deep and swim'?"

Van Gogh shrugged. "To move on? That makes the most sense."

I nodded, agreeing that in the context of this card, that explanation did make the most sense, but I couldn't help wondering what Mom meant when she'd said the phrase to me because I didn't know the context, at least not one that I could decipher.

"Do you think that's why she left? Because she couldn't?" I asked, closing the card and placing it in the box.

"Maybe," Van Gogh said, sighing. He gave way to a dry cough, untwisting the cap of the water bottle to drink the rest of the water. I could see him purposely swallowing a few times after he finished the water to suppress an encore.

I wanted to tell him to just cough, as I could see him struggling to hide his cold, but I understood his strategy. If he started openly coughing and one of the conductors or passengers heard it, they'd likely grow suspicious and probably think he had COVID-19. If they suspected he'd contracted the virus, then it was very possible we would be removed from the train. If this happened, then I had no idea how we would ever make it to New York. We didn't have enough money to buy another two train tickets, and there was no way that we could walk there. This train was our last resort.

"Maybe," Van Gogh repeated, "but I doubt it because she left in 2009 and this letter was written in 2007. If she left because she had a miscarriage, she would have left earlier."

"True, but Grandma Rose did say that losing a baby is traumatizing and leaves scars 'in your bones, in your soul,' to quote her," I noted. Although I didn't have an eidetic memory, I did have a knack for memorizing most of what I read, especially when I *just* read it. "It's possible she never got over the pain and just couldn't look at us anymore."

"It's possible, but doubtful," Van Gogh asserted, gingerly taking the card and rereading it to himself. After he finished rereading the card, he placed it back on my tray and pointed to the paragraph that referenced Marilynn. "It's possible that Aunt Marilynn's death had a negative effect on everyone. She was hospitalized, so she obviously died from her sickness."

"It doesn't sound like Grandma Rose was healthy either," I noted, pointing to where she mentions her health. "What do you think it was?"

Van Gogh shrugged and leaned back.

"I'm not sure," Van Gogh stated. "Maybe just age."

I reread the card to glean any additional insight into Mom's family, but it was to no avail. All that was revealed was that Marilynn died from some illness, Mom was devastated by her miscarriage, and that Dad wanted her to move on from her grief.

"Hey, that's something!" I exclaimed. "Maybe that was the impetus for her running away. I mean, you know how insistent Dad could be— maybe it just pushed her over the edge. In one of the cards, Grandma Rose mentioned that they were having issues, but she really didn't go into it. Maybe this opened the rift that much more. What do you think?"

Van Gogh continued to lean back, now with his head tilted down, his chin resting on his chest. He was probably looking at some indiscriminate spot on the floor, pondering my question.

After what felt like a minute or so, I asked Van Gogh my question again, but he didn't respond. I reached over and carefully lifted up his sunglasses to see that his eyes were closed. I gently lowered his sunglasses, making sure they were securely on the bridge of his nose, and I placed the cards back in the box.

Even though we still had two cards left to read, it felt wrong to read them without Van Gogh. If we were going to gain more insight into our mom and her family, we needed to do it together. I still didn't know how what we'd learned so far would help us convince her to take us in, but knowing something about her—other than the fact that she ran away from us—had to be helpful in some way or another.

Closing our mom's box, I looked out the window to find the sun dipping into a bath of auburn and gold rays among the sea of light blue. My eyelids suddenly felt heavy, as though Van Gogh's exhaustion was contagious. Similar to my brother, I leaned back and let myself dissolve into the darkness behind my closed eyelids.

The reverberation of the slam vibrated in my bones, but I couldn't detect where it came from. It was a pulsating feeling that settled within me, but I could not find its source.

"Say goodbye to your brother," a voice hissed. Its sinister tone slithered down my spine as I remembered the gray coffin, which suddenly manifested in the room.

I opened my mouth to scream, and although I felt my throat tense and my vocal cords sizzling with the exertion of my scream, all I heard was silence. I closed my mouth and tried again, to no avail. My sound was locked within me.

Gripping the sides of my head, my fingers dug into my scalp as I sank to the floor. My descent was endless as I felt like my knees would never reach the surface.

"Say goodbye to your brother," the voice maliciously whispered. It felt like his words had a vampiric quality, as if the sound of his words had the malevolent ability to suck the life force out of me.

I continued to sink, hearing the words repeating.

I began to dissect them, as if by deconstructing the sentence I could find some sense.

"Say," the voice said—but I could not say anything. This was a dare to do the impossible. Silence was not a refuge, but a prison. "Goodbye" offered a sense of finality, a generic parting, an end to a conversation—a pleasantry to only intensify the horrific moment. "Good" ceased to exist; there was only a biting "bye." The "good" left to mock me. "To" was the preposition expressing direction in a rudderless boat on the River Styx. "Your" was a singular ownership, an attachment to what has been stolen from me. "Brother," my only brother, my only family, taken from me, locked away in a gray coffin.

Put it together.

Say goodbye to your brother.

A mockery of what I could not do, what I could no longer find, and who I'd lost.

"Now you've got it!" the disembodied voice bellowed.

Despite understanding its uselessness, I fought through the silence, fought through the descent, and attempted to respond, attempted to ascend.

My muscles were jelly and my tendons were broken, withering rubber bands, losing their elasticity. My voice was only a memory, as I continued to mouth, "No!"

Just as I felt myself losing the battle, I heard the honeyed whisper. At first, I couldn't discern what it said, but the tones grew more distinct, firmer.

"Just breathe deep and swim," the other voice encouraged. It was soft, and its warmth cracked the steely, frozen darkness.

"Just breathe deep and swim," I repeated back to myself.

Before the other malicious, mocking voice said anything, I took a much-needed deep breath as I leaned forward and swam into nothingness, toward the gray coffin.

Without a word, I flipped the lid open, revealing untouched matching gray satin but no body, no brother. The hollowness was almost comforting until I heard it, a sound akin to chalk and sandpaper mixed together, merged to form something new, something simultaneously familiar and unfamiliar. However, the louder it grew, the more it clouded my vision. Gray and white fog heavily descended over the gray coffin as the sound became more distinct, more recognizable.

I felt myself shoot up while still sitting. It took me a moment to recognize where I was—still on the train. But I no longer felt the motions of its movement. I looked out the window to see a sign that read "Petersburg." For a moment I thought we were in Russia before I realized that we had stopped at one of the stations on our way to Penn Station.

I leaned back and looked over to see Van Gogh's chin still resting on his chest. His body shuddered with the muffled dry coughs, which were increasing in frequency. I hated to wake him, but I knew that if I didn't, people would begin to pick up on the coughing and someone may call the conductor over.

"Van Gogh," I said groggily, giving his shoulder a nudge. "Van Gogh, wake up." I gave his shoulder another nudge as he lifted his chin from his chest. His cough persisted, but he turned toward me, sunglasses and cap still firmly in place.

"Are you okay?" I couldn't help asking.

He nodded, coughing. I scanned our surroundings from my seat. Some heads began to turn in our direction as Van Gogh continued to cough.

He must have sensed people beginning to look at him, as he quickly shot up and went into the bathroom.

⁓⊱◈⊰⁓

"Breathe deep and swim," the honeyed voice whispered.

I scanned my surroundings, only making out gray smears on white walls. I stood in the middle of the cylindrical room, searching for something.

"Breathe deep and swim," the voice repeated, except this time the tone was more distinct, more insistent, as if it were giving me a directive.

"What do you mean?" I heard myself ask, and then jumped a bit at hearing the sound of my own voice. "Where are you?" I asked, turning to see no one.

"Breathe deep!" the voice exclaimed. "And swim."

"Why do you keep saying that?" I pleaded, still feeling the urge to search for something. I had no idea what I was trying to find, but it felt lost. I felt lost. "Where are you?"

I waited for a response, but I did so in vain because the voice didn't respond. I intently listened for a breath, anticipating some noise, some direction, some insight into who was speaking to me, but I was confronted with the blaring silence.

"Who are—" Before I could even finish the question, a flash of recognition ignited my neurons. It was at that moment that I knew who was speaking to me. I knew what I was searching for but could not find.

"Where is the coffin, Mom?" I asked. I continued to search but to no avail.

"Coffin!" an echo exclaimed. I didn't know who created that echo, but the voice was not mine.

"Coffin?" a voice questioned, except this voice was different. There was no malicious intent, and it didn't have a honeyed tone. "Young man, is your friend coughing?" I thought I heard the voice ask again.

"What?" I asked, sitting up in my seat. It took me a moment to readjust to reality, especially with my sunglasses on, creating the illusion that it was the middle of the night.

"Is your friend coughing?" the voice asked again, to which I turned to face the conductor who had checked our tickets, who was standing beside my brother's empty seat, pointing toward the closed bathroom door. "He has been in there for quite some time, and the other passengers have expressed concerns. It sounds like he is coughing in there."

"Oh," I said simply, not knowing what else to say. *Think, think, think.* I knew if I mentioned that Van Gogh had a cold that this would raise suspicions, so I needed to think of another excuse. *Why else would he be coughing for an extended period of time?* I didn't even know how long he'd been in the bathroom, so my excuse needed to cover any length of time. I wished that Van Gogh would come out of the bathroom, as he was so much better at coming up with excuses than I was. *What would Van Gogh say? Think, think, but don't overthink.*

"It's the mask," I lied. "It's causing him to cough and he didn't want to bother the other passengers, so he went into the bathroom."

The conductor furrowed his brow as he looked from me to the bathroom and back to me again.

"Does he have asthma?" the conductor asked.

"Actually, yes," I said, remembering that Sophie would occasionally cough under her mask because it was one of the symptoms of her asthma.

"He should try using Pulmicort. That's helped my sister—she also has asthma," the conductor stated.

"Yes," I quickly said. "I'll let him know when he comes out."

The conductor nodded, but he didn't move from his spot. He continued to look at me with his furrowed brow.

"Any reason why you and your friend are wearing sunglasses on the train? It's not that bright in here."

"It helps us sleep," I lied again, feeling a little more on edge, as well as surprised that I came up with an excuse that quickly.

"Well, it's daytime, you don't need those anymore," the conductor noted.

Reluctantly, I pulled off my sunglasses, and placed them on my tray, which I had never put up before I fell asleep.

The conductor studied what he could see of my face.

"I swear, you look familiar," the conductor observed, "but I just can't place you."

"I guess I just have one of those faces," I suggested, feeling compelled to smile underneath my mask.

The conductor paused for a moment before turning to leave. "I hope that your friend feels better."

I nodded and continued to smile, watching him go, terrified he might turn back at any moment. After about a minute, sensing that the conductor was out of sight, I leaned back in my seat, picked up Mom's box and my sunglasses, and put my tray up so that I could stand up.

Holding both the box and my sunglasses, I stood up and took a few steps toward the bathroom door, where I could hear the muffled sounds of my brother's coughing.

Gently, I knocked on the door.

"Van Gogh, it's me. Let me in," I said to the closed door.

The door quickly slid open, and a hand reached out and pulled me into the tiny room.

Still wearing his sunglasses and cap, Van Gogh stood a few centimeters away from me, holding his mask over his mouth.

"Why would you say my name? Do you want to get caught?" he asked, coughing in between words.

"I'm sorry, but you know people can hear you coughing in here, right?" I whispered, hoping that no one could hear our conversation. "That conductor, the one who checked out tickets earlier, came by and asked if you were okay."

"What did you say?" Van Gogh whispered.

"At first I didn't know what to say, but I eventually said that the mask was causing you to cough, which kind of led to you having asthma—so if anyone asks, you have asthma."

He fitted his mask back on his face, nodding. "Got it. Wait, why aren't you wearing your sunglasses?"

I tucked my sunglasses into my front pocket. "The conductor asked why we were wearing sunglasses. He started to become suspicious, so I had to take them off. It is a little weird to be wearing them inside. I don't think anyone will recognize us if they just see our eyes." I didn't dare tell him the conductor thought I looked familiar. I knew if I did, Van Gogh would either make us keep our sunglasses on, which would be even more suspicious, or he would make us get off the train.

Nodding, Van Gogh gingerly took his sunglasses off to reveal darkening circles underneath his lackluster lily-pad-green eyes.

"Damn," I unintentionally whispered, realizing that my brother probably had more than just a simple cold.

FOURTEEN

DEFIANCE

My legs were stiff from sitting for so long, but I knew we would be arriving at our destination soon. But "soon" really couldn't come soon enough as Van Gogh's coughing persisted. He continued to drink water to clear his throat but it didn't really help, and he was no longer able to control when and how often he coughed.

When the passengers would turn their heads and narrow their eyes, looking at us suspiciously, I would point to Van Gogh and say, "Asthma." He also seemed to be breathing a bit louder and heavier to keep up the ruse.

After he'd emptied his third water bottle, I offered to get him another one, but he just shook his head. He also refused to eat any food, saying he just wasn't hungry.

The urge to ask him if he was okay kept reentering my thoughts, cast by the ebb and flow of worry and fear. I could no longer suppress that disquieting thought that my brother was *really* sick. It was at times like these that my phone felt like a phantom limb; I kept reaching into my pocket, searching for it so that I could look up his symptoms, to only find my sunglasses.

I couldn't say I didn't suspect he had contracted the coronavirus because he *had* taken care of our dad when he was sick, but I *knew* that Van Gogh had been so careful. I unintentionally shook my head, as if I could shake this notion out of my mind.

He will be fine, I kept telling myself. *He's Van Gogh, he'll figure something out.*

"Hey!" Van Gogh exclaimed. "Aren't there more letters?"

I looked down at my hands, which were still clutching our mom's box.

"Yeah, but I think we'll be in New York soon," I noted.

"We have time for one more," Van Gogh pressed, struggling to sit up in his seat while motioning for me to pull down my tray.

With my tray down, I placed the box on top, and pulled out the second to last unread card. Once again, the envelope read "Happy Anniversary" on the cover, with clipart of a smiling bride and groom atop a pastel, five-tiered wedding cake.

February 2nd, 2008
Dear Ann,

Happy Tenth Anniversary, and happy second birthday to Wolfgang! This is definitely a milestone, and that much more special because you have two blessings in one to celebrate. I know that your tenth may, by far, feel much different than your first anniversary, but it is just as special. I also know you have experienced several hardships— but treasure moments like these, where you can celebrate with your loved ones. Thank you again for sending me pictures of Wolfgang, Van Gogh, and Benjamin. The one that Benjamin took of you reading a book to your boys was precious. It's the one that I keep by my bedside, along with the pictures of you, Marilynn, and Alan.

Alan said he really enjoyed his visit with you. It was so fortunate that he and Alice were able to see you during the holidays. Of course, I missed having my family around for Christmas, but with Alan and Alice now living in the same building as me, we were just an elevator ride away from one another.

To respond to the question in your last letter, they are still trying to have a child, but unfortunately, they have not been successful just yet. I told your brother not to lose hope as they have only been trying for a few months. As you know, your brother loves working with kids, which is one of the reasons why he chose to be an elementary school art teacher. You should hear him talk about his students. He is so passionate about teaching. It was for this reason that I told him to stay in Queens, so he could be close to his school, but he insisted on moving back to the Bronx to be close to me. I have to admit, I did not put up much of a fight. You know I wish we could all be together in one home, but I know you each have your own lives. I hope that one day soon you, Benjamin, and the boys can come to the Bronx.

However, until then, have a wonderful, beautiful wedding anniversary, my little Ann. I also want many pictures of Wolfgang on his birthday!

Love Always,
Mom

As I placed the card back into the box, I turned to Van Gogh, whose eyes were closed.

"Van Gogh, are you awake?" I questioned, noticing that ever since he'd come out of the bathroom, he had been drifting off. I wished he would just allow himself to sleep for a few hours, maybe it would help.

"Yes, I'm awake," he muttered.

"Did you read the whole card?" I asked, picking the card back out of the box, and placing it back on the tray.

"Let me read the last lines," he said as he flipped open the card. After a few seconds, he closed it and gestured for me to place it back inside the box.

"Do you remember ever seeing Uncle Alan?" I asked, closing the box.

Van Gogh leaned back in his seat, and closed his eyes. I thought he was drifting off again, until he said, "I don't remember him. I mean, he does look familiar but that's only because he looks so much like Mom and a lot like you."

"He does?" I asked as I opened the box and pulled out the wedding party photo. I looked again at the taller man standing to the left of our mom. His high cheekbones did mirror mine, as did his light-blue eyes and light-brown hair, except his was a lot shorter, so I couldn't tell whether or not it was wavy.

"Aside from his height," Van Gogh began, pausing to cough, "you two are practically carbon copies."

As I looked from our mom to the rest of her family, I could not deny the resemblance.

"In fact, you look more like him"—Van Gogh began again, interrupted by another cough—"than you do our own dad."

"Well, if I am a carbon copy of Uncle Alan, then—" I began before I was cut off by Van Gogh.

"Don't finish that thought," he barked, turning to me with his dim lily-pad-green eyes. As I looked into his cloudy eyes, I could hear my wave of worry slap the sandy surface once again. I swallowed the urge to communicate my concerns to my brother because I knew he would try to assuage my fears. Instead, I turned away from him and looked out the window to observe the smears of auburn and golden autumn trees as we flew down the track toward our destination.

"Okay, how about this thought then," I began, still looking out the window. "Maybe I look like Uncle Alan, but he is an artist, like you."

"I guess," I heard Van Gogh mutter. I waited for him to continue, but all I heard was another dry cough, so I went on instead.

"Also, we don't know whether or not he married Alice, but we *do* know that they were trying to have a child together, so we might have a cousin! Plus, in 2008 he was living in the Bronx with Grandma Rose, so if Mom is in the Bronx, maybe we will also meet Grandma Rose, Uncle Alan, Alice, and possibly a cousin."

I turned away from the window to look down at the closed box. I was tempted to reopen it and read the last card, but my peripheral vision revealed that Van Gogh had drifted off again. He didn't nap for too long, though, as he jumped up a second later when he heard the conductor announce, "Next stop, Penn Station!"

᷊᷋᷼

As we entered the dark tunnel, I shimmied past my brother to put our mom's keepsake box in my backpack, instead of back into his. Before I could sit back down, the conductor who had checked our tickets walked toward me. He gestured for me to come to him. I stood in the aisle, unable to move but unable to sit down either. I looked at Van Gogh, who had nodded off once again. Just like a deer caught in the headlights, I merely stood there, watching the conductor gesture to me one more time. When he realized I wasn't walking over to him, he walked over, and stopped only inches away from me and looked down at Van Gogh. He furrowed his brows and then stared at me for a moment before he reached up and pulled down our backpacks.

As he handed me the backpacks, he lowered his voice to say, "Look, I know what asthma looks like, and your friend does *not* have asthma."

I turned to Van Gogh to see him shudder every time he coughed, which had become more frequent in such a short amount of time.

"My brother is fine," I muttered, immediately regretting my statement. Even though I didn't reveal Van Gogh's name or any other identifiable information, I knew that divulging *any* information would already be *too much*.

"Son, your brother looks very sick," the conductor asserted. He immediately lowered his voice so that he was practically whispering. "I don't know what your brother has, but you need to get him to a hospital immediately, because he may have … you know. Normally, I would escort you off of the train to protect the other passengers. You and he are lucky this is your stop."

I nodded, wondering how lucky we could possibly be—being orphans whose only hope was to find a mother who may or may not be in the Bronx, and who, if we did find her, may or may not take us in.

Since the conductor wasn't moving, I said, "Yes, I understand, and I promise that he will get checked out."

The conductor turned to leave, but before he left, he uttered, "There is an Urgent Care on 33rd, near Penn Station. Try getting him there."

I nodded in response. Seemingly satisfied with this, the conductor walked down the aisle and into another car.

As I stood in the aisle, I couldn't help but breathe a sigh of relief as I felt the train slowing to a stop. Firmly shaking Van Gogh's shoulder, I told him we'd arrived. He slowly opened his eyes and squinted up at me.

He gripped the armchair to stand up, but as soon as he stood, he fell back into his seat. My heart rate began to pick up as he shook his head and attempted to stand up once again, but to no avail. He whispered, "Give me a minute," as I tried to flatten myself as much as possible so that the other passengers could pass by.

Even though I shut my eyes, and my back was to the other passengers, I could feel them glaring at my brother as they slowly walked by us. As soon as I didn't feel anyone moving by, I offered Van Gogh my arm.

"Here, lean on me," I said, as Van Gogh gripped my arm and pulled himself up, finally standing.

The tunnel felt endless, most likely because Van Gogh was walking like he was making his way through quicksand. The neon lights seemed to pulsate as people passed us by. Occasionally, someone would look back to see my taller brother with his right arm wrapped around my shoulders. I tried to just focus on the path that would take us to the exit. However, I couldn't help but notice their glares and whispers as they were probably asking one another what we were doing and questioning what was wrong with my brother.

Although my brother was thin, between his weight and the heft of our backpacks—mine slung over my shoulders and his that I was gripping in my right hand—I struggled to stay upright. *Just keep going. You'll make it, you have to,* I kept saying to myself as I looked toward the exit, feeling that they were just within reach.

As we struggled toward the exit, Van Gogh didn't say a word, but he did put his sunglasses back on. Although the conductor never placed us—or if he did, he didn't mention it—I understood why Van Gogh wanted to disguise himself. He didn't direct me to put mine on as well. I didn't know if that was because he could barely speak without coughing, or if he was just too tired to give any orders. Either way, I was grateful because those sunglasses would have made it that much more arduous to make our way through this tunnel.

Just keep going, I kept repeating to myself every time I felt a wave of exhaustion overtake me. *Van Gogh would do the same for you, just keep going.* However, I would undercut this perseverance with the truth: *Van Gogh is different. He can do anything. I don't have the stamina, I am not Van Gogh.* Confronted with this reality, I paused, feeling as if my knees were going to buckle, but somehow the other voice came back, stating, *Tough. Go.*

"Breathe deep and swim," I uttered to no one as I took a much-needed deep breath and kept moving forward.

I continued on in this way until I reached the end of the tunnel. It couldn't have been a more glorious sight, as Van Gogh and I stepped out into what looked like a grand hall. I took another deep breath and slowly exhaled as we continued to move forward.

We were soon confronted by passengers who were either wheeling their suitcases toward their track, standing in the hall looking down at their phones, or staring up at the glowing black Departures board.

As I scanned the area, I adjusted my backpack.

"Where should we go?" I asked Van Gogh, whose head was tilted up, probably looking up at the Departures board. We both scanned the board looking for "the Bronx," but I didn't see any trains destined for this borough. However, what I did see was a Customer Service station. Without saying anything to Van Gogh, I walked us toward the booth.

The line was short and evenly spaced, six feet apart—or at least that's what the floor stickers indicated. However, the wait was not long, and the person behind the plexiglass soon asked, "How can I help you?" into her microphone, which I heard through the speakers embedded into the plexiglass shield.

"We're trying to get to the Bronx, specifically Pelham Parkway. Is there a train that we can take from here?"

The woman typed on her keyboard for a moment, and then said something about the Number 2 train. I nodded, but before I could ask Van Gogh for the money, he reached into his wallet and started to slide the money in the plexiglass opening—but the woman held her hand up.

"You will need to get a transit card in the station. To get to Pelham Parkway, you need to take the MTA Number 2 train. In order to do that, you have to exit this station and then go to Penn Station on 34th St, where you will take the Number 2 train, Northbound to Pelham Parkway," she explained.

"When will the train leave?" I asked, holding onto the tickets she had slid through the plexiglass opening.

"They usually run every ten minutes, but they are sometimes delayed. You'll just have to wait on the platform."

Before I could thank the woman, she asked, "Is your friend okay?"

"Yes, his leg is just stiff from the trip," I lied quickly. I couldn't help but wonder how many times I would have to make up excuses for my brother's appearance.

The woman nodded, apparently believing me. She provided us with directions to the Number 2 train, for which I thanked her. As we continued to move through the station, I noticed a waiting area filled with empty seats. Although I knew that Van Gogh wanted to go to find our mom as soon as possible, I desperately needed to sit.

Without even asking him, I sat us both down in two empty seats. I placed Van Gogh's backpack next to me.

"Why are we stopping?" he asked, taking his sunglasses off just to rub his eyes. He quickly put them back on as he turned to me.

"My legs are cramping up," I said, lying again. "Plus, the train is supposed to run every ten minutes or so, so we won't miss it. We have time." Although this was the truth, I knew that Van Gogh probably would've been more comfortable being much closer to our train, as it was going to be quite a walk to get there.

"In the meantime," I began, unzipping my backpack to pull out our mom's box, and then rezipping my backpack and placing it back on my shoulders, "we can read the last letter."

I gently pulled out the only card that we hadn't read. Its cover was a pale gray, devoid of any greeting or inscription to mark the occasion.

When I opened the card, a torn envelope fell out. In the center, I saw our address written in our grandma's penmanship. My eyes drifted to the left-hand corner, where I found what must have been my grandma's address, "*760 Pelham Parkway, Bronx, NY 10462.*" I tucked the envelope into my pocket, ensuring that I had it on hand. If we couldn't find our mom, maybe we could find our grandma at this address. It seemed that she was living there for a while, and she and our mom had kept in touch, so if our mom didn't live in the Bronx, maybe our grandma could point us in the right direction.

Before reading the card, I scanned the script, noticing that this card was dated March 27th, 2009—the year that our mom left us.

March 27th, 2009
Dear Ann,

You may wonder why I am writing to you now, especially after our phone conversation. I know that I said very little as I was trying to process everything that you said. Once again, words failed me in the moment, but hopefully they will not fail me now. I know that it is difficult for you to speak to Benjamin and the boys, but I think that you need to tell them. Ann, they have a right to know. However, I know that you are going to do what you want to do.

In response to your question, of course you can come home. You do not have to ask. This is your home as much as it is mine. I love you so much Ann, and desperately want to see you, but I wish that you would speak to your family before making any decisions.

Love Always,
Mom

"She went back. Maybe we will find her on Pelham Parkway," I said, turning toward Van Gogh, who was leaning back in the chair. That was when I heard him gasping for air.

I felt the box and the card slip from my hands as I listened to my brother struggle to breathe. He kept gripping his throat as he arched his back in the seat.

"Van Gogh!" I shouted as I pulled his mask down to help him breathe. I couldn't think of anything else to do other than to rid him of the mask that may have been an obstruction. As soon as I lowered the mask, I was confronted by his blue-tinted lips and pale skin. His nostrils flared and he continued to gasp as I helplessly sat there.

What would Van Gogh do? What would Van Gogh do? What would Van Gogh do? The question played on repeat with no answer in sight. I had no response, no solution because I was not my brother. Because I could not follow his instincts, I had to follow my own.

"Help!" I screamed as loudly as possible. "My brother can't breathe! Call 911! Please, anyone!" The few people who were also seated in the waiting area, as well as those in the periphery, began to form a circle around us. While some held up their phones to take a picture, a few began punching something into their phones.

As I scanned the crowd—some observers and some who were holding their phones up to their ears speaking to someone on the other line—I pleaded to anyone who would listen.

"Please, help us. Please!" I shouted. Before I could continue, I felt a hand grab my shirt. I turned to face Van Gogh, who was shaking his head while still struggling to breathe. Decidedly, I pulled off his sunglasses to see his widening lily-pad-green eyes practically screaming as loudly as I had been shouting just a moment ago.

"I don't care!" I yelled at Van Gogh. I could hear my voice crack. I swallowed hard before continuing, "You're going to the hospital!"

Without even waiting for Van Gogh's response, I turned back to the crowd. Before I could even say anything, a man who was holding up his phone stepped out of the crowd, but kept his distance as he exclaimed, "I called 911. They should be here soon."

I nodded and mouthed, "Thank you." I could barely see the man as my vision became blurred from the watery walls forming over my eyes. I quickly wiped the tears away with the sleeve of my shirt, but a new wall just formed in its place, so I just let the tears run down my cheeks.

Even though Van Gogh was still shaking his head at me, I stared steadily into his eyes.

"You're not going to die," I promised. "You need to trust me. Do you trust me?"

My brother didn't nod, shake his head, or even acknowledge that he'd heard me. I didn't know whether or not he was considering this question. Like it or not, he needed to trust my instincts in that moment, as I had always trusted him, no matter what.

FIFTEEN

FEARING THE PAST TENSE

Van Gogh was strapped to the gurney with an oxygen mask secured to his face by one of the EMTs. Each EMT was hidden behind an N95 mask, goggles, and a translucent plastic outfit that was cinched around the waist with a thin strap and that covered their uniform. The EMT who placed the oxygen mask on Van Gogh asked me if I suspected that my brother had COVID-19. Without even looking at Van Gogh, I looked straight into the EMT's eyes and nodded. Even though I didn't want to admit that my brother had probably contracted the virus, most likely from our dad, I knew I had to acknowledge this truth. I didn't know whether or not Van Gogh could hear us, but I knew that if he could, if he *did* hear us, he would be angry with me.

Van Gogh vigorously shaking his head played on repeat in my mind. In response, I shook my head, as if my mind were an Etch A Sketch and I could merely shake a memory out of existence.

"The man who called in described the symptoms, but he was unsure about whether or not he suspected that your friend had COVID-19, so we came prepared," the EMT told me.

"He's my brother," I asserted as another EMT walked to the other side of the gurney.

"Ready, Tony?" the other EMT asked, to which the EMT who was talking to me turned away to nod. They flipped something underneath, which allowed them to lower the gurney to the floor, and lift my brother into the back of the ambulance.

"I want to go with him," I insisted, walking toward the open ambulance door as they secured my brother's gurney into place. One of the EMTs, assumedly the driver, walked around to the driver's side door. Tony looked to his partner, who was climbing into the back.

Before he could respond, I begged, "Please, I *need* to go with him." I could feel my voice cracking again, so I swallowed hard and tried again. "I can't leave him. I *won't* leave him!" I didn't even realize that my hands were clenched into fists at my sides until the EMT gestured for me to climb into the back, and I unclenched my hands to grab onto the door to pull myself up—which normally would have been easier to do without my backpack weighing me down.

As I sat on the bench, I eased my backpack off of my shoulders and placed it on the floor between my feet. Tony moved between my brother's gurney and me to reach for the double doors, pulling them closed. As soon as the doors were shut and locked into place, the sirens blared in rhythmic, blasting whirls of sound as we raced down the road.

Everything felt so surreal as we pulled into the ambulance bay. Tony and the other EMTs swiftly but carefully got my brother out of the ambulance, and then raised the gurney once it was on the ground.

I quickly grabbed my backpack and followed my brother and the EMTs. Without stopping, Tony yelled back to me, "We're taking you and your brother to get tested!"

I nodded as I quickened my pace. Although I didn't feel sick, I knew those with the virus could be asymptomatic. Plus, I'd hardly left Van Gogh's side throughout our trip, so it was possible that I had contracted it as well. However, I did not care. Whether or not I had also contracted COVID-19 was of no concern to me; in fact, if I could make an exchange, myself for Van Gogh, I would in a second. *Please live, please live, please live*, I pleaded. My new thought was now on replay as we entered the COVID-19 triage tent.

A healthcare worker, who was also adorned in an N95 mask, goggles, and a white translucent plastic outfit that was cinched around the waist, held up long cotton swabs. She explained to me that she was going to insert one swab into each nostril to retrieve a sample to determine if I had the coronavirus.

I could barely hear myself say "okay" as she lowered my mask, and inserted the first swab into my nostril. As she moved the swab around the inside of my nose, I scanned the area for my brother's gurney, but all I could see was an endless sea of clinicians dressed in white plastic outfits, goggles, and N95 masks.

"Where is my brother?" I asked, as she pulled the swab out of my nostril and placed it into a cylindrical tube that she capped with a stopper.

"Who is your brother?" she asked as she inserted the next swab into my other nostril.

"He was on a gurney. He was wheeled in here by EMTs wearing the same outfit that you have on," I said in an unusually nasal voice.

"PPE," she corrected. "Did you two come together?"

I nodded as she took the second swab out of my nostril and placed it in an identical cylindrical tube.

"Well, if you are being tested, I am sure that he is too," she stated as she pulled my mask back up.

I nodded as she turned away to hand the tubes to another clinician. I scanned the crowd once again, wishing that Van Gogh were wearing something that set him apart from the crowd, but that wish was made in vain as I still could not place him.

I gripped the strap of my backpack as I waited, frozen in place until the clinician who took my sample told me to follow her.

∽∾ᖇᘓ∾∽

Every sound was simultaneously muffled and deafening. However, distinguishing one sound from another was not high on my priority list as I processed the information that I received. I wasn't even sure who communicated what information to me. Initially, I only heard snippets of words and phrases. I tried to piece it together into a comprehensible and cohesive thought, but I was too exhausted to try.

Positive. Negative. Built-up antibodies.

"What does that mean?" I asked.

One of the clinicians—who, I do not even know—explained that the other test they gave me indicated that I had *had* the virus but now I did not.

"I had the virus," I muttered to myself.

Apparently, I'd been asymptomatic. I was able to survive this devastating virus without even knowing that I had *had* it. It invaded both my body as well as my brother's, but it had chosen to try to destroy my brother.

"Why not me instead? Take me instead," I bargained with no one. I considered this to be a necessary exchange as I couldn't imagine a world without my brother.

Oxygen mask. Convalescent plasma. COVID-Only ICU. No visitors.

The "no visitors" phrase stuck and reverberated in my mind as I sat in a chair, waiting for someone—I had no idea who—to come speak to me. As I waited, I unzipped my backpack, which I had placed on the floor between my feet. I rifled through paperback after paperback, searching for our mom's box but to no avail.

That is when I saw the flash of the box and all of our mom's mementos—our grandma's cards, our mom's wedding photos, and our hospital bracelets—falling to the Penn Station floor. I squeezed my eyes shut as my stomach sank at the thought of the box lying beside the train station's chairs.

As I opened my eyes to gaze at the hazy, darkening sky, I knew that the box had either been swept up or taken by someone who might find some use in a used keepsake box. Either way, I knew that I would never see it again.

I leaned back in the chair and closed my eyes once again.

꩜

"Hello?" I heard a voice say. It was gentle yet firm. "Are you awake?"

I felt like I was peeling open my eyelids, but I reluctantly did so to face a woman, slightly taller than me, wearing a N95 mask and PPE. She sat beside me, positioning a clipboard on her crossed legs.

Her hazel eyes were exuding sympathy, as I could see her hesitating to put her gloved hand on my shoulder. Similar to her hand, our instincts to offer physical comfort retracted in times like these.

Instead, she used her hand to scribble something onto her clipboard.

"My name is Carol. I am a social worker at the hospital, and I am here to help you," she stated, a string of platitudes that she must make to all of the minors she ended up working with. "I know this must be a difficult time for you, Wolfgang."

I nodded, only to belatedly realize she'd mentioned my *name*.

My head turned in her direction so fast, I practically gave myself whiplash. "How do you know my name?"

When asked about any identifiable information by a clinician, a nurse, an EMT, any member of the hospital, I'd only said that my brother was sick. I'd refused to tell anyone our names, so how was it possible that this woman knew my name? I looked down at my backpack to see if my name was written anywhere on the outside, but the canvas was free of ink.

She blinked a few times before responding, as if she were considering whether or not she should tell me the truth. She then reached into her bag to pull out an iPad that she moved closer to me.

The screen lit up with the steady image of Van Gogh aiming our dad's shotgun at the gas station thief. I swallowed hard, feeling that my voice would crack if I attempted to speak. Fresh tears stung my lower eyelids as I watched Van Gogh, so confident and so seemingly healthy, ready to protect me. Van Gogh was always there to protect me, and yet I could not protect him from this stupid, deadly virus.

I turned away from the screen, feeling the tears well up.

"The video went viral," Carol explained as she turned off the iPad. "It was a local news report, but it obviously got a lot of attention. Your brother, Van Gogh, is very brave."

I nodded. I couldn't help but wonder if people would begin to use the past tense to describe my brother's bravery, to describe any aspect of my brother. Van Gogh *was* brave, Van Gogh *was* determined, Van Gogh *was* my brother.

Although he wasn't on a ventilator, he was seriously ill. Hundreds of thousands of people succumbed to this virus. He didn't have any preexisting conditions, and he was only sixteen years old, but young, healthy people died from this virus practically every day.

Van Gogh *was* safe. Van Gogh *could not* contract the virus, not him. He *was* too strong, too vital … and yet, somehow, he had.

I closed my eyes and took a deep breath before turning back toward her.

"Yes," I asserted. I took another deep breath before asking the obvious question, "Now what?"

"Now, we need to contact someone, a legal guardian. If you don't have a legal guardian, we will need to call social services," Carol explained.

At the mention of social services, I jumped in my seat. That's when I heard the slight crinkle of the opened envelope in my pocket.

"We have a legal guardian," I told her as I pulled out the envelope to show her our grandma's address. "I don't have our mom's phone number because my cell phone broke, but I have our grandma's address."

Carol gingerly took the envelope from me and examined the address.

"Is this your grandma or your mom?" she asked, looking at my grandma's name in the upper left-hand corner of the envelope.

"It's my grandma's, but my mom lives with her," I explained with such certainty in my tone. I had no idea how I mustered up that false conviction. Maybe it came out of a longing for that assertion to be true. However, if our mom were no longer living with our grandma, then at least our grandma would be at that address.

What if she isn't there? I thought, the slither of doubt creeping into my mind. *What then?*

"My uncle is also there," I continued. "His name is Alan Miller. My mom is Ann Miller, and my grandma is Rose Miller, as you see on the envelope."

Carol nodded, jotting something on her clipboard.

"We will try to get in touch with your family," she said with assurance saturating her tone.

Before she could get up to leave, I exclaimed, "Wait, can I make a call? A different call? There is someone close to my brother who needs to know what is happening."

Carol looked down at the iPad as she gestured for me to take it.

"This is a hospital-issued iPad," she explained. "Let me know when you are done." I didn't know if she was breaking hospital protocol, but either way, I was grateful.

Although it was late, I hoped it was not too late to take this call.

I only heard a couple of rings before I heard, "Hello, who is this?"

"Hi," I nervously stated, and then quickly cleared my throat. "Hi, Janelle, it's Wolfgang." Aside from our home phone, Van Gogh's cell phone number and mine, Janelle's was the only other number that I had memorized.

"Wolfgang!" she exclaimed. "How are you? How is Van Gogh? I couldn't believe it when I saw you both on the news! Do you know that footage of Van Gogh in the gas station went viral?"

Although we weren't on FaceTime, I looked away from the iPad when Janelle asked if Van Gogh was okay. Instead, I avoided that question and responded to her last.

"Yeah, that's what I've been told," I admitted.

"How did this happen?"

Just breathe deep and swim, I told myself. I took a deep breath before stating, "It's a really long story, but I think that you should know."

I managed to condense days of our escapade into under an hour. I struggled to steady my tone when I explained why I was calling her from a hospital.

"Jeez," she exclaimed, "I have no idea what to say."

I took another much-needed deep breath before simply saying, "Yeah."

"So," she began, then paused. I could hear her take a deep breath as well. "So, is he—I mean, have you seen him yet?"

I shook my head, and then told her that visitors were not allowed to see patients in the COVID-Only ICU. Without her even finishing her thought, I knew that she was going to ask me if Van Gogh was going to be okay, but I think she knew I couldn't answer that question.

"Janelle," I said more seriously, getting to the *real* reason why I had called. "Why did you break up with Van Gogh? I mean, he told me what you said, but you know that our dad wouldn't have been an issue. Van Gogh didn't agree with him at all, and he was willing to do anything, even leave our family to be with you."

She didn't say anything for a moment, as if she was contemplating exactly what she wanted to say.

"Wolfgang, I loved Van Gogh. I *still* love him, but his proposal would not have worked. He said that he would run away. Actually, he said that the both of you would run away. And when he says something, he means it. That's one of the things that I love about him, but I could never ask him to do that. I could never ask him to uproot you, and to abandon your dad just to be with me. I knew he was more than willing—determined, actually—to make that sacrifice, but I couldn't let him do that. It would've been wrong. Do you understand?"

I nodded, the sacrifices that Van Gogh made for me practically slapping me upside my head. I cringed at their memory, feeling remorse and regret cover me like a heavy blanket.

"Yes," I managed to say, feeling tears stinging my eyes again.

"You need to be there for your family, through anything. Even though your dad was a racist, he was still your dad. I would not allow Van Gogh to choose me over his family, so I did what I thought was right. I let him go. I let *us* go," she concluded.

"Thank you for telling me," I said. I could always rely on Janelle for her honesty and candor, even when the truth was difficult to hear. However, I couldn't help but wonder where we would be if Janelle *hadn't* broken up with Van Gogh. Would we still have traveled to the Northeast to find our mom who abandoned us when we were little? Would our dad have died sooner if Van Gogh had not been around to care for him? Would Van Gogh be in this hospital right now, fighting for his life?

Before I could even work through these unanswerable questions, out of the corner of my eye I saw Carol walking toward me.

"I think I have to go," I said to Janelle. Before she could respond, I hung up.

I shut off the iPad as Carol once again sat in the chair next to me.

SIXTEEN

SOMETHING TO TELL YOU

"Hi, Wolfgang," Carol said as she carefully placed her clipboard on her lap. It was covered in incomprehensible scribblings that were akin to the English language. Maybe doctors weren't the only ones who were notorious for their poor penmanship. Perhaps if you worked anywhere around medical professionals, your handwriting would suffer.

"Unfortunately," she continued, beginning with the somber, ominous adverb, "we were unable to get in contact with your mom or your grandma. In fact, neither a Rose nor an Ann Miller lives at that address." Before continuing, she flipped the front page of her clipboard to review something she had written.

At that moment, I didn't know exactly how to feel. It was a mixture of disbelief and expectation, a cocktail of contradictory emotions. Even though Grandma Rose's last card revealed that our mom ran back to her childhood home, that was eleven years ago. It was difficult to believe that she would remain in the same place for over a decade. Perhaps she traveled to another state and she convinced her mom to move with her. They could literally be anywhere now, and I had no way of finding her.

I waited for Carol to look up, expecting her to tell me what Van Gogh and I dreaded: that social services would place us in foster homes. Well, they would place *me* in a foster home. At this time, there was no way that they could place Van Gogh.

I closed my eyes to concentrate on swallowing the stinging lump forming in my throat at the thought of being separated from Van Gogh.

It seemed like a lifetime later, but Carol finally turned away from her chart to look at me.

"However," she began with an adverb that signified hope, "we were able to get in contact with Alan Miller, who lives at the address you gave me."

"My uncle. Really?" I said in disbelief, feeling myself sit up a little straighter.

"Yes, he said that he would be here as soon as possible," Carol confirmed.

Maybe all hope was not lost just yet. I was biologically tethered to at least one person living in New York, maybe more if he and Alice were finally able to conceive. Perhaps Uncle Alan knew where we could find our mom. Perhaps he could help us get one step closer to home. I just needed to know that Van Gogh could move with me, that he would be all right, otherwise it was all for naught. If he didn't make it, if Van Gogh didn't survive this, then they could do whatever they wanted with me.

If not for my brother, I would have never made this trip. If not for him, I wouldn't have cared if social services put me in an abusive, neglectful, or compassionate foster home. It wouldn't have mattered, none of it, without my brother.

As Carol got up to leave, I asked, "Can I speak to Van Gogh? I mean, I know that I cannot see him but is there some way that I can call him?"

Carol tilted her head and looked at me with that sympathetic gaze that people give you when you're truly pitiful, and that indeed described my current situation.

"Yes," Carol uttered. "I will make the arrangements. We can give your brother an iPad so that you can both speak to one another. He is wearing an oxygen mask right now, so it may be difficult for him to talk, but he will be able to hear you. I'll let you know when he wakes up so the two of you can speak. In the meantime, stay here. I will come get you once your uncle arrives."

∽◈∾

With nothing left to do other than wallow in my horrendous circumstances, I decided to distract myself by reading Arthur Miller's play, *All My Sons*. I'd reached the scene where Chris was confessing to Ann that he felt a kind of responsibility to his fellow soldiers that had sacrificed themselves in World War II.

Although I wasn't a soldier, Chris's sentiments resonated with me. Similar to Chris, Van Gogh was consistently weighed down by his responsibility for me. Pangs of guilt pummeled me as I reflected on how this sense of responsibility resulted in him contracting the virus. If Van Gogh didn't care about me, then maybe Janelle wouldn't have broken up with my brother. He would have told her that he was leaving and wouldn't have even mentioned taking me. Maybe that would've changed her mind. Yes, he would still cut ties with our dad, but I wouldn't be uprooted. Maybe that would have changed things. I would be firmly planted in place, and maybe that very fact would have changed Janelle's mind. Even if it hadn't, maybe Van Gogh would have pursued her after she ended their relationship because he wouldn't have anything holding him back. He would have been tethered to her and nothing else. Maybe, if Van Gogh didn't feel responsible for me, then maybe he would have emancipated himself.

I was drowning in this sea of "maybes" that could never be. Those alternative paths only existed in the past. I knew it was useless to pick up the thread of any of these "maybes" because they led to potential, unknown paths. However, I couldn't help myself. My guilt was too raw, too palpable. Perhaps it was a form of self-punishment to consider these "maybes," but this understanding didn't deter me, so I continued to think through these potential realities until Carol came back and gestured for me to follow her.

Carol led me to another waiting area with similar chairs, where a tall man with eyes like mine and wavy brown hair stood. Although his N95 mask covered the lower half of his face, he looked exactly like my mom's wedding party photo counterpart.

My uncle's eyes quickly scanned me as his cheekbones rose, indicating that he was smiling from underneath his mask.

"Wolfgang," he stated in disbelief. "I can't believe it." Although we were separated by six feet of space, I heard him so distinctly that it was as if he was standing a few inches away.

"You can both speak in here," Carol said, gesturing to chairs that were probably six feet apart. "I will leave you two to talk."

I thought as soon as Carol left that a flood of questions would flood out of my mouth, but I could barely vocalize a single one. I just sat with my backpack once again firmly between my feet, staring at the uncle I'd never known I had.

"Wolfgang," he said once again, except this time his tone was softer, more affirming. "I really cannot believe that it's you. Your mom showed me pictures, but that was when you were a baby. I just cannot believe how much you have grown, and how much you resemble her."

"Where is she?" I blurted out. I jumped a little, surprised by my own bluntness, but it was the question that I needed to ask. It was the sole reason why we were in this state.

I knew that he would be taken aback by my question. I thought that maybe he would even be reluctant to reveal her location. *Did he warn her that we were here? If so, why isn't she here? Does that mean she doesn't want to see us? Does that mean that she does not want to see her dying eldest son?*

Before I could work myself up, I noticed my uncle lowering his head to look down at his Keds. I saw him take an unusually long, deep breath before he exhaled.

"Wolfgang, she didn't want me to tell you this, but I knew it would come out eventually. The truth usually does," he stated, looking up to make eye contact with me. "Wolfgang, your mom passed away eleven years ago."

"What?" The question practically fell out of my mouth as I processed what my uncle told me. *Our mom was dead? She had died eleven years ago?* I could only process these thoughts as questions as the certainty of their truth sank in.

"Yes," he choked, and then took another deep breath before continuing, "Your mom never wanted you or Van Gogh to know this, but you need to know. The reason why your mom left you, Van Gogh, and your father is because she had pancreatic cancer."

"She didn't leave because of Dad?" I asked, recalling her annotation in *Madame Bovary*, where she wrote my dad's name next to Emma Bovary's realization that she was disillusioned by the prospect of love, and that marriage was not bliss.

In response, my uncle shook his head.

"Did Dad know?" I asked, to which my uncle shook his head again.

"No. Although she and your dad didn't always get along, she loved him. She loved you all so much that she didn't want you to suffer from watching her die, and she *knew* that she was dying."

Anger welled up inside of me as I listened to my uncle.

"She did not want us to *suffer*?" I yelled, surprising myself with my volume but continuing anyway. "What did she think leaving us with no explanation would do—make us *happy*? My dad was miserable and bitter! He died thinking that his wife left him, not knowing why. My brother—who is fighting for his life right now—and I traveled from Florida to New York just to find a woman who didn't even have the decency to tell us the truth!"

My uncle didn't move to leave, nor did he refute my statements. He just continued to sit in the chair and take in my anger. I knew that my wrath was misdirected but I couldn't help it. I was usually the calm one, the cautious one, the understanding one, but I was so tired of filling that role. Faced with my mom's selfish choice, all I could do was yell at my uncle because the person I really wanted to yell at had perished.

"I know," Uncle Alan acknowledged, nodding. "You have every right to be angry. I never agreed with her choice to leave you. I told her that she *should* tell Ben, that she needed to allow him to grieve, and that she should be with you and Van Gogh in her last moments of life, but my sister always did what she wanted. She was so stubborn."

He paused, perhaps to provide me with an opportunity to respond, but when I didn't, he went on.

"Maybe I should have defied her and contacted you all, but it was her life, not mine. I needed to respect her wishes, even after she died.

However, even though I didn't agree with her decision, I do know that she did it out of love. She loved you all *so much*. I actually think her choice to leave you was the most difficult decision that she ever made. When I would visit her and Mom, Ann cried practically every day," he stated, pausing for a moment to wipe away the tears that began to form in the corners of his eyes.

I took this moment to ask, "What did Grandma Rose think about this?" I couldn't even fathom why that mattered, but I needed to know. I was tired of the secrets; I needed to know everything and anything.

Another deep breath before a response was provided. "She didn't agree, but she also respected Ann's wishes. She knew that she was losing another daughter to cancer. She didn't want anything to taint her last moments with Ann because maybe she knew they were her last moments as well."

"What do you mean?"

"Our mom had a heart condition. She passed away soon after Ann died," my uncle stated grimly.

"She *died*?" I asked in disbelief.

Even though I only have one memory of my mom and literally no recollection of my aunt and grandma, their loss felt like the weight of shouldering a backpack filled with stones. I sank in my seat, resigning myself to the fact that my life was being invaded by death. It was as if every single family member was a piece of fruit hanging from a tree, falling after their ripeness speedily turned to rot. *Is Van Gogh next?* I thought as I imagined his ripe fruit forming dark-brown blotches on the peel.

"Yes," Uncle Alan acknowledged. "She had been sick for a long time, but after Ann died, she went downhill very fast. I think that she died of a broken heart, and losing her husband and two daughters was more than her heart could take."

"What about you?" I couldn't help but ask.

"Me?" my uncle said, pointing at himself. "I had come back to take care of Mom—"

"I know," I interrupted, to which Uncle Alan raised an eyebrow, puzzled by my assertion. "I found Grandma Rose's cards. Mom kept some, one in which Grandma Rose mentioned that you came back to the Bronx to be closer to her. That's how the hospital found you. Mom kept one of the envelopes with her—*your*—address on it."

Uncle Alan nodded, and then continued. "Well, then you know that I came back to take care of my mom. When Ann came, she stayed in my mom's apartment, our old home."

"Why did you stay?" I asked.

"You know, I asked myself that exact same question for a while. You would think that I would have moved back to Queens with Alice, but we were already settled in our apartment. Plus, Alice got a job as a dental assistant in a practice that is very close to our apartment complex, so we stayed. Also, even though I know that my family is gone, that apartment complex is still my home."

I swallowed hard, longing to call some place *home*. The only home I'd ever had was with a person who needed an oxygen mask to breathe. At the thought of Van Gogh, my eyes welled up with tears, so I turned away.

"Wolfgang, I know that this must be so hard to hear, especially with Van Gogh being…" He let his voice trail off. We both knew that what he was going to say didn't need to be said out loud. Instead, he ran his fingers through his hair and sighed. "I know this is hard, and I know I should have told you this long ago. The only thing I can say is that I'm sorry."

I nodded, looking down at my backpack, picturing Van Gogh's backpack and our mom's keepsake box abandoned in Penn Station. I had nothing to offer my brother, no hopeful news about our mom, no positive news about his own health—I couldn't even offer him the bare necessities that he'd packed in his backpack. I had nothing left to give. I was useless, helpless.

"However, there is more that I can *do*," my uncle went on. "When I moved back home, Alice and I rented a two-bedroom apartment in hopes that we would have a child, but we never did. So, we don't need two rooms—we only need one for ourselves. I have already discussed this with Alice, and we both want the two of you to live with us."

At the words "live with us," I jerked my head up and stared into my uncle's eyes.

"Really? Both of us?" I asked in disbelief. I seemed to be in a constant state of disbelief that evening. "But Van Gogh—" I began, but before I could continue, my uncle held up his hand.

"When Van Gogh gets better, he can come stay with us. We have a pull-out couch that converts into a bed, so you may have to stay there while Van Gogh isolates in the bedroom. Once he's better, we will move you in. What do you say?"

When. My thoughts lingered on that word. I wished that this expectation were true because I couldn't imagine a world where Van Gogh wasn't alive. I had already lost so many people I never knew, and our dad who never sought to really know me. I just couldn't lose Van Gogh too. I didn't know if I could ever survive that loss.

"I need to talk to Van Gogh first. He needs to know about our mom," I replied, standing up and holding the hospital's iPad.

It took some time to set up, but finally I saw an image of my brother with a thick plastic mask over his face. Although the mask kept fogging up every time he breathed, and my brother was framed by white machines with blinking lights, I was grateful to just see him alive.

"We have someone who can speak for you brother, just in case it becomes too strenuous for him to speak without the mask," Carol indicated.

"Thank you," I said, turning to her. "Um, do you mind if I am alone?" I asked, to which she nodded and said to call her when we were finished. She walked into the hall, where she spoke to my uncle.

Turning back toward the screen, I said, "Hi, Van Gogh." I cringed at my simple greeting. *What are you going to say next, "How are you?"*

Van Gogh lowered the oxygen mask to speak. Although his voice was low and raspy, I was still able to understand him. "Wolfgang," he said, pausing to lick his dry lips. "Are you okay?"

I was dumbfounded by his question. Was *I* okay? He was the one struggling to breathe, hooked up to an EKG and who knows what else, and he was checking to see if *I* was all right?

"Why does that matter? I mean, you're the one who's hospitalized. Am *I* okay?" I answered, sounding irater than I'd intended to. "I'm sorry, I don't know what's wrong with me. I didn't mean it."

"It's okay, I get it," my brother noted, the words followed by a series of dry coughing.

I cleared my throat before continuing.

"Van Gogh, I am so sorry. I know you didn't want to go to the hospital. I just couldn't—" I felt myself choking on the burning lump forming in my throat. "I just couldn't let you die. You're my brother, my only family—I just couldn't."

Van Gogh pulled up his oxygen mask to take a few deep breaths before he lowered it again to speak.

"I know why you did it. You did the right thing. I know I always ask you if you trust me, but you should trust *yourself*. And, in response to your question—yes, Wolfgang, I trust you. I will always trust you." He let a series of dry coughs escape before lifting up his oxygen mask once again.

I allowed my tears to stream down my face as I listened to my brother. Even though nothing was resolved in that moment, I somehow felt lighter, better, as if his trust in me would help us both get through this horrific storm.

"Van Gogh," I began, and took a much-needed deep breath of my own before I said, "I have something to tell you. It's not going to be easy to hear, but you need to know. It's about Mom."

SEVENTEEN

FINDING HOME

The graveyard was covered in a sheet of snow with tufts of yellowing brittle grass poking through. The gray clouds hung low in the sky, with the promise of new snow. Stray flakes began to dance in the air as I brushed the layer of snow off of the tombstone. The trees stood bare and their branches were like spindly fingers, reaching for the sky. Their nakedness contrasted the speckled dying fauna that adorned the graveyard, placed in remembrance for the dead who would never watch their flowers wilt and decompose to match their now dead bodies.

"Here lies Van Gogh. He was a kind and brave soul, who was truly a national hero. He will truly be missed."

"Very funny," I said sarcastically, holding smooth stones in my hand, ready to place them on the grave site.

Van Gogh lowered his N95 mask to smirk at me.

"Look, if you can't eulogize yourself then who will?" he teased, giving my shoulder a playful nudge. "Plus, without our original birth certificates, who can even prove that we are alive?"

I cringed, flashing to the image of Van Gogh's abandoned backpack at Penn Station. Days after he was hospitalized, Uncle Alan and I went back to Penn Station to find his lost backpack and Mom's keepsake box, but to no avail. When I told my uncle that our birth certificates were in

Van Gogh's backpack, he assured me that we could order copies. Although this didn't make up for the loss, it was certainly a relief to hear.

"You have a warped sense of humor. How do you think Janelle would take that joke?" I asked.

Van Gogh ran his fingers through his hair before securing his mask back on his face. "She'd probably kill me, so then I would need it."

"A self-fulfilling prophecy," I teased.

Placing one stone on our mom's grave and another on our grandparents' tombstones, I said, "Uncle Alan was right—stones make way more sense than flowers."

I even placed a stone on our dad's tombstone. Uncle Alan had arranged for his body to be flown in from Florida, so that he could be buried next to Mom. Even though our dad never forgave our mom for running away, it was obvious that he did love her, and deserved to be by her side for eternity.

Van Gogh nodded, placing his stones on our grandparents' and our parents' tombstones as well. We then placed the rest of our stones on our Aunt Marilynn's and our other relatives' tombstones.

As we stood up to look down at the chiseled gray slabs that signified where our relatives' bones would rest forever, Van Gogh placed his hand on my shoulder.

"I'm sorry," he said sincerely. "I know these past few months have been especially hard on you. I didn't mean anything by it."

"I know," I said, moving closer to my brother so that I could wrap my arm around his shoulders. "These past few months have been hard on everyone, but especially you."

Van Gogh hadn't been released from the hospital until right before Halloween, when he'd no longer needed an oxygen mask to breathe. However, even though he spent over a month in the hospital, I'd continued to speak to him every day. In fact, Uncle Alan bought us both cell phones just so that we could communicate with one another while Van Gogh was in the COVID-Only ICU section of the hospital. As soon as I could, I also gave Janelle the number. Although she didn't call Van Gogh as often as I did, she called enough that they could begin to reconcile. She even promised to visit us in New York once the vaccine was given to the public.

When my brother was feeling up to it, Uncle Alan even gave him his own iPad so that he could participate in online classes. Although our uncle still had to go in to work to teach in a hybrid classroom setting, the school we were enrolled in had remote learning. I wished that our uncle would look for a position where he could also teach remotely, but he loved his current school.

We were all extremely careful so that we wouldn't contract the virus. Even when Van Gogh came to live in the apartment, he remained in isolation until he tested negative.

Practically everyone, including myself, thought that Van Gogh may not make it—but in the end, it didn't surprise me that he did. I should've known he would survive because he was a fighter. If Van Gogh wanted something, then he would find some way to get it. If Van Gogh wanted to live, then he would. It was that simple. It might not make sense, but then again, not everything that my brother did made a lot of sense.

Before we turned to leave, I scanned the tombstones once more, relieved to see the absence of my brother's name.

As we walked toward our Aunt Alice's car, who was waiting for us, I said, "I can't believe that Uncle Alan and Aunt Alice just invited us to live with them—just like that."

"I can," Van Gogh replied confidently. "I knew that if our relatives saw us, that would be enough to convince them."

I would've refuted Van Gogh's statement, but I knew that he was right. However, I also think we were incredibly fortunate that our uncle and aunt were kind, generous people. Even though the plan had been to find our mom, we found the next best thing—a loving extended family. Sometimes, you just need to go with the flow.

You just need to breathe deep and swim until you find the shore.

ABOUT THE AUTHOR

Jenna Marcus is an academic leader and published author of the YA novel, *My Unusual Talent*. She has a fervent passion for leveraging her decade of expertise to robustly enhance and redefine the quality of teaching and learning. As an avid reader, she believes that every child should find a book to love. In her current position as a Reading Interventionist at Harlem Village Academy-East Middle, a charter school that practices progressive education, she seeks to imbue a passion for reading in her students. This is one of the primary reasons she writes Young Adult fiction, so that our young people can discover stories that they relate to and/or that inspire them to read.

Until June 2020, she held the combined roles of Director of Student Achievement and IGCSE Coordinator at the private international boarding school EF Academy in New York. In addition to her professional experience, she holds a MS. ED in Educational Leadership, a MS. ED in Middle Childhood & Adolescent English Education and a BA in Literature; she is also a certified in School Building Leadership and ELA. Currently, she lives in New Rochelle, NY.